IN ANOTHER WORLD

IN ANOTHER WORLD

Yolisa Baduza

Published through:
Parexcellence Publishing House
www.parexcellencesa.co.za
office@parexcellencesa.co.za

Editor: Pale Baduza

Contents

DEDICATION

This book is dedicated to the Almighty God whom I serve and who delivered it to me through a dream. He has been with me in my hopelessness and in my joy. In every step I have taken on this journey we call life, He has carried me, all the way. Every breath I take is through His undeniable strength, mercy, and love. I lost hope more times than I can remember, and each time, He helped me to find it again. This book was written for everyone who has shed innumerable tears and been beaten down by life, so they may believe that in the darkest moments there is always hope in the God who can do the impossible. You are loved and never forgotten.

Chapter **1**

Adam

Adam watched his wife sleeping. She looked so beautiful, so peaceful. He slowly moved closer to her ear and whispered, "Babe, why don't you leave me? You know I am not good for you. Why do you stay?" He slipped inside the covers with his wife and laid his head on the headboard. He was fiddling with his fingers. "I slept with Anna today." Adam was speaking to his wife, Sarah, as if she were awake. "You know Anna. She works at the pharmacy on Palm Street. Well anyway, I slept with her. I knew it was wrong when I did it. I knew it was going to hurt you, but I did it anyway. I just had to have her, hun, I could not help myself." No woman could resist his green piercing eyes, dark brown hair and muscular, athletic body. He was a very handsome forty-year-old man and he used it to his advantage. "I tell myself I am going to change. I try to resist, stay at home with you, but it's like something pushes me to be the worst Adam I can be. The one who cheats on you. Who never touches you and breaks your heart every chance he can. I know deep inside I can be better. I know there is a better person inside of me. If only I can reach in and grab him. I am destroying us, I feel trapped, and I need help Sarah," he said sadly.

In the depths of torment, his eyes watered, and he wept silently until he realized Sarah was stirring and starting to wake up. She opened her blue eyes, took one look at his face, and realized he had been crying.

"Adam what's wrong?" she said with concern. She reached out for his hand but Adam moved quickly from the bed and out of the door, leaving his wife all alone. She screamed after him, "Adam please don't go! We never talk anymore!" Her screams turned into tears. Adam was standing behind the door and heard every word. He was listening to her crying.

"Yes, we do," he said under his breath with his palm against the door. "When you are sleeping that's when we talk," he murmured. He slowly kissed the door as if it were Sarah and regretfully walked out of the house, hoping, and praying he didn't meet temptation on his way to the bar.

Chapter 1

Sarah

Sarah cried and cried, until she tired and drifted off to sleep. When she woke up the next day, she tied her long, beautiful blond hair into a ponytail, covered her slim body with her gown and went out of her bedroom. She was a thirty-year-old woman, slightly haggard from years of stressing and emotional suffering. Her once bright brown eyes lacked spark and her naturally striking looks were jaded in a manner you sensed but couldn't quite describe. She had not lost her beauty. It simply no longer shone through, like an unpolished jewel. She walked straight to the kitchen and grabbed the phone on the wall in anguish then dialled her mother's number. She tapped her right foot impatiently, waiting for her mother to answer the phone. Finally, it was picked up.

"Mom....," Sarah cried into the phone.

"Sarah darling what's wrong?" her mother asked in a worried but knowing tone. "It's that God forsaken son-in-law of mine again, isn't it!" she shouted into the phone. "Sarah for the life of me, I don't know why you won't just leave him. You know he has slept with half the town, and you just take it!" Sarah could not take it anymore.

"Mother, I didn't call for a lecture! I just need someone to talk to. Please, mom, don't judge me now. Please just listen," she said desperately, and her mother went silent and listened. She took a deep breath and began to speak again. "I know he is cheating on me! The whole town is talking about it. Everywhere I go people are pointing at me." Her tears would not stop falling as she carried on speaking. "The girl at the pharmacy can't even look at me because of guilt. You know I sometimes wonder when the girls greet me in town, if they have slept with Adam. Everywhere I go I have those thoughts, Mom. Even when I am in church, I wonder who will be his next conquest. Is there any woman in this town who hasn't slept with my husband?" Almost shouting in exasperation, she opened the kitchen cabinet and took out a packet of chocolates. It was the only thing she and her husband still shared; the love of chocolates, especially the one called *Destiny*. They loved the name. *How ironic she surmised*. Ripping the packet open she started eating the chocolate ravenously like a mad woman.

"Then what kind of life is that my darling?" her mother asked hesitantly. "I am sorry I screamed at you. It's just that I love you and I hate what this boy is doing to you." Sarah's tears started again.

"Mom, it's like a disease that I can't find a cure for. I love him too much."

"Love is not supposed to make you sad, Sarah."

"I tried to leave him," Sarah replied as she took another big bite of the chocolate. She leaned into the wall and slid down into a heap on the floor. "I packed my bags and walked out of the house. I was determined never to come back, but in a week there I was!" she laughed, mocking herself. "I could not breathe without him. I love him so much that it is killing me. I don't understand it myself. My love for Adam is keeping me in a cold and lonely marriage. I am in pain, Mother. All the time! I feel like I'm in a cage. I am a joke to

him, to this town, and to myself!'' she wept hysterically, throwing the chocolate onto the floor. Sarah's mother responded gently.
"It's going to be alright darling. There has to be a way out of this. As long as there is a God there has to be a way out of this. I wish I could be there right now and hold you in my arms sweetheart."

"Mom,'' Sarah said in a childlike voice.
"Yes dear,'' She answered tenderly.

"Do you still pray for me?''

"Every day."

"I love you, Mom."

"I love you too, sweetheart."

"I have to go now, but can we pray together?" Sarah asked.

"OK darling let's call God into the situation, we are in need of His mercy. Dear Father, please hear Sarah's cries. We ask you, Lord to shine your light upon this dark situation and help my daughter. She needs you now more than ever. Please guide her, strengthen her, and walk beside her through this difficult time,"

"Yes, Lord.'' Sarah continued, "You are my only hope now."

"We ask this Lord in Jesus' name, Amen''

Adam

"Goodbye Mom, I love you."

"Goodbye, sweetheart. Love you too," her mother responded gently.
She lovingly kissed the earpiece and cut the call.

James

James was looking at himself in the mirror. He was a very tall, athletic man, bordering on lanky, with well-defined muscles. Many women found him attractive though, and called him "Brown Sugar" behind his back, with his fair brown skin and lazy, sexy black eyes.

How had it all gone so wrong in his life? When had he lost control of it? He wondered to himself. 'Had it all started when his mother died or was it before then? Was his life destined to fail before he was born? Had the gods create a life so unsatisfying that the only way he could stand it, was to be angry all the time?' He was brought back to reality by the knock at the door.

"James, we are running late!" his father yelled in irritation.

James opened the bathroom door and humbly apologized to his dad. "Sorry Pops, I didn't notice how late it was."

"You are supposed to be on top of things. Running a veterinary surgery is no child's play. I need to know that you are going to be on top of things when you take over. You can't be my assistant forever. Shape up, man!" His father was as domineering as ever.

"Yes sir," He replied dejectedly. James survived the day by doing what he always did, following his father's instructions to the tee, counting the hours till he got off work. At five he hastily called out to his dad, while walking out of the door. "Dad, I am off to see Melanie." Without waiting for a response, he was out of the door.

Melanie was James' escape from his life of misery. They both knew it was just physical. But she was manipulative. She always made sure she got what she wanted, whatever the cost. James, too desperate to escape his world, never allowed himself to see who she really was. He needed her.

He drove to the restaurant where she worked and found her waiting outside the restaurant. Melanie was an attractive, busty brunette with big brown eyes and a slender body who never missed a chance to show off her well-endowed cleavage. She kept her hair in a bob cut.

"Well, it's about time you showed up!" she yelled at him.

"Get in!" James yelled back. He was in a bad mood.

"Having a bad day I see, what did Daddy dearest do this time?" she got into the car, mocking him. "Anyway, we need to talk" she continued, but James silently drove off. "Fine, we will talk at the hotel."

Adam

As soon as they received their room key from the receptionist, James pulled Melanie by the hand. He was clearly on a mission and dragged her from the hallway till they reached the hotel room. He was all over her, the minute they were in the room. He started kissing her violently.

"Stop!" she shouted.

James was surprised by her outburst. "What's the matter babe?"

"We need to talk," there was a determined look on her face. "I don't know how to tell you this, so I will just tell you. I am pregnant," she said without flinching.

"What!" he blurted. He could not believe what he was hearing. "I thought you were on the pill?" he didn't hide the note of accusation.

"I *am* on the pill, but it's not a hundred percent," a thought started forming in her mind. "We could get married," she said with a smile.

"Huh!" James laughed nervously and without any thought for Melanie's feelings, "Mel, we don't even love each other! Besides, what about going to Art school and pursuing your dream of being an artist?" Melanie was starting to get annoyed. James was not taking her news too kindly and Art school was a touchy subject. He knew better than to bring it up, she thought to herself.
"If I was meant to be an artist, I would have been born into a wealthy family which could take me to an art school, but instead I am pregnant and a dirt-poor waitress!" she shouted back. James was

surprised at her response and staggered back to the edge of the bed. Toning her voice down, Melanie walked over to him and putting her arms around his neck, continued in her manipulative way, "We are good together babe and that's enough for me." James peeled her hands off. He stood up with a determined look on his face.

"What about what I want Mel? You can give up on your dream but I am not ready to give up on mine." Rage was starting to well up in Melanie. If James was thinking of dumping her with a baby, he had another think coming, she thought to herself.

"James you are never going to do anything with your music. And I am never going to be an artist!" She realized from the look on his face that she had hurt him in the most horrible way. She was slowly removing what little hope James was carrying in his heart piece by piece. It was the only way to get what she wanted. One has to lose for another to win, that's life, she figured. Coldly, she aimed her words straight at his heart. Going for the kill, she said, "If it was meant to be, it would not be so difficult to achieve. Maybe life is trying to tell us something. Some dreams are not meant to come true James Have you thought about that?"

James felt as if someone had hit him with a rock. How can she be so cruel? He thought to himself. He had known that this day would come. The day when his inner thoughts and fears would be spoken out loud by someone. Today Melanie was saying those exact words. The small inner voice inside told him not to give up, reminding him of the promise he made to his mother to never give up on his dreams. Melanie needed to be encouraged that's all. 'She just needs to be encouraged not to lose hope,' he thought to himself. James sat her on the edge of the bed next to himself.

He said with a reassuring smile on his face, "Mel what if it's not supposed to be easy? Maybe we are meant to fight harder and a little longer."

It was time to pull out the big guns. Melanie knew James could never stand to disappoint anyone. That's the reason he was still under his father's thumb. If guilt was the only way to keep James, so be it. Crocodile tears appeared in her eyes.

"Grow up James! I've been fighting one obstacle after the other my whole life. I work hard at that restaurant and still don't have enough for tuition. Now I am pregnant! How am I supposed to fight that? I am tired and I can't fight anymore!" She started crying hysterically. "You go ahead! Leave me with your baby and go after your dreams, you selfish fool! I guess I will be the responsible one," she ended in a broken tone. James knew deep down that Melanie was right. What kind of man would he be if he left her with a baby? He had to do the right thing, the responsible thing.

"You're right Mel," he said with a dismayed look on his face. "Its time I accept things as they are. You're pregnant." He laughed piteously, "I will be there for you and the baby. I don't mean to sound insensitive, it's just that I always thought I was meant for more. I guess I was wrong." Melanie had won and she knew it. Trying to hide the smile on her face she softened her tone.

Chapter 1

"So, what are we you going to do?"

"Get married I guess," James replied.

She had won, James had buckled. "You promise you won't change your mind?"

"I promise." He said shaking his head despondently

She didn't need to be there anymore. "Look I can see you need time to absorb all of this, so I am going to leave. I will get a taxi home," she chirped triumphantly.

James didn't say a word as he watched her walk out of the room. Driving back home, he found himself praying. 'God if you are there, please don't let me end up like this!' He kept repeating the prayer over and over in his mind, feeling helpless, and more lost than ever.

Jessica

Jessica was watching the sunset from her porch. It had been a beautiful day and she was enjoying her favourite slab of chocolate, *Destiny*. The sky was painted in beautiful colours of red and yellow that almost brought tears to her eyes. She was interrupted by Derrick tapping her shoulder. Derrick was attractive. He was the bald, tall dark type. He had a well-manicured beard and strong presence; the sort of presence that made him stand out in a room. He had an average physique that was a chiselled muscular body in his younger days. He had now let himself go a little, leaving him just well-proportioned.

Adam

"Gazing at the sky I see," he said smiling, "what are you thinking?"

"Oh, nothing in particular, just looking at the sunset." Jessica threw away the chocolate wrap in the trash can.

"Why do you like this chocolate so much?" he asked.

She smiled, "It's delicious and because of its philosophical name."

"Shall we go?" he took her by the hand, leading her to his silver Bentley Continental GT very expensive car. They had dinner reservations at the town restaurant. Derrick was an affluent, successful man, and town lawyer. They had been dating for six months. He was the town "catch" and he knew it. The restaurant was not crowded on a Monday night. It was dimly lit allowing customers some privacy and the waitress gave them the table by the window. Derrick the charmer moved the seat for Jessica and waited till she sat down before he sat opposite her.

"Did I tell you how beautiful you look tonight," he said taking her hand and kissing it.

"No, you didn't, but thank you," she teased.
"So, sweetness, did you think about what we discussed?" he asked with a cunning smile.

"Can we order first, before we start talking about that?" she stalled.

Derrick, feeling offended, snapped back, "I don't think a marriage proposal can be described as *that!*" He used his fingers as inverted commas.
Jessica was suddenly not enjoying herself at all. She wished she was anywhere in the world but there.

"Your proposal comes with a condition." She avoided looking at him and fidgeted with her fork.

"A very reasonable condition," He replied sternly, taking the fork from her hand. Jessica slowly looked up and was met by a stony look on the face of the man sitting across from her. 'He is angry,' she mused. Derrick was being unfair and very insensitive, and she was starting to get annoyed.

"Not to me it's not!" she shot back defensively. Incensed by the fact that she had raised her voice, he was just about to answer her when they were interrupted by the waiter.

"Uh, can I have your order," the waiter said, looking at Jessica. 'What a stunning lady!' the young waiter thought to himself. The couple restrained themselves in front of the waiter. The young gentleman noticed that he had interrupted a heated argument and started feeling nervous.

"Yes," Jessica said oblivious of her beauty and how she made men feel She had long, soft, black, hair that flowed down in opulent curls to her shoulders, complimented by bold, beautiful, thick eyelashes and large dark eyes which carried a hint of pain; a voluptuous, curvaceous black woman with an hour-glass figure. "I will have the chicken salad with apple juice."

"And I will have a steak, rice, vegetables and a glass of beer," Derrick replied as he looked at the young gentleman. He knew the very thoughts the young gentleman was having about his date. Giving him a sharp look that said 'back off! This one is mine!' The waiter realized he was caught. He clearly got the message and quickly left. "I am offering you a good deal here sweetness. We both know there aren't many single men in town making good money," Derrick continued proudly. Jessica could not believe how arrogant he could be. "You can have a husband, children and never work at that silly little children's school ever again," he scoffed.

"I happen to like my job," she said proudly. She started getting annoyed again. "Sleep with you or else it's over, is not a marriage proposal! It's an ultimatum. And I don't like ultimatums! Not from you! Not from anyone!"

Derrick interrupted her. "Lower your voice; we are in a public place," he said discreetly, seething with anger. Aggravated, he moved closer and whispered in irritation, "I am not being difficult; we have been dating for six months! And I have waited long enough!" Jessica started to feel ambushed by him. She was not going to take it.

"You know my beliefs," she shot back. "I want to be intimate with somebody only when I am married to them." Derrick interrupted her impatiently. "Yes, yes but I *am* going to marry you! I mean surely

15

you can't be questioning my intentions and feelings for you?" he replied accusingly. He was trying not to lose it completely, but she was not making it easy for him.

"I have kept myself for thirty-one years! You knew that when we got involved. I am a Christian and....," she said with passion. Derrick interrupted her before she could finish speaking.

"Don't tell me about being a Christian!" he said, boiling. "Most of the girls in church have relations with their husbands before getting a ring on their finger! Society in general accepts it. Your best friend Donna slept with Mike before *they* got married," he ventured firmly. She opened her mouth to reply but Derrick raised his hand to stop her. Trying to get a hold of himself, he said gently, "and I believe that as adults we need to have that physical connection before we get married."

Jessica, fiercely determined to stick by her beliefs, said, "That's what you, society and Donna believe, but not me!"

Derrick, losing control, hissed "That's why you are still single at thirty-one! Every man you meet hits the road when they hear that nonsense!" Jessica, floored, could not say anything. He had pulled the rug completely out from under her.

"It's not nonsense!" she cried in torment "how dare you!" Tears formed at the corners of her eyes. "The fact that you don't believe in my principles, does not give you the right to insult them nor me!"

she said hotly. Grabbing her purse, she sprang up, but Derrick caught her hand.

"Please don't go." He regretted hurting her. 'But it had to be done' he schemed to himself.

"Let go of me!" Jessica sobbed.

"You're right, I am *so* sorry! Please don't leave," he pleaded. "look our food is coming."

The waiter placed the food on the table and retreated without even looking at them. Derrick started to wipe the tears from her face and tenderly placed his hands on both her arms, gently pushing her back onto her seat.

Jessica spoke slowly, "What you said was cruel. And hurtful."

He got up from his seat, walked to her and knelt down. "This is not going to be easy to hear but believe me it's for your own good. All I ask is that you keep an open mind and listen to me before you say anything." he asked lovingly. Jessica nodded. She didn't have any more fight in her. Derrick had given her a heavy blow. "As beautiful as your beliefs are, they are not for this generation. They are from the past. They have left you with nothing but loneliness." He looked her straight in the eye. She started crying because she had been so lonely for so many years. Derrick saw that what he was saying was beginning to make painful sense to her. He continued, "I didn't leave like the rest of the men in your life. I stayed and bent over backwards for you. I could have gone to someone else." Seeing the hurt in Jessica's eyes, he tried to make light of the situation by cracking a joke. "I just want to taste the milk before I buy the cow," he said with a smile. Jessica laughed through her tears.

"You have been so good to me, but I thought you understood. Did you think you could change me when so many failed?"
He started to stroke her face and said, "I did understand, but I thought since I am going to marry you, it would change things." He continued, smoothly in his loving tone, "I am different, baby. I am not just after your body; I want to marry you."

"I know," Jessica replied with tears running down her face, "but I have always dreamed of giving myself to my husband on my wedding night. You are asking me to give you something so precious to me. You want me to give up on my dream."

"Yes, I am," Derrick said, selfishly. He was on a mission and oblivious to anyone else's feelings but his own. They did not call him a great lawyer for nothing, he thought to himself. "But I promise you," he said with a smile on his face, "I will be there the next day and the day after that AND the day after that." 'I'm on a roll. He thought to himself. The forty-one-year-old knew exactly how to use his silver tongue to his advantage. "I will take you away from a life of loneliness," he promised. Slowly he started kissing her on the right cheek. "I know you are lonely and dying to be loved passionately," he said as he nibbled her left ear, "don't pretend, you know I am making sense" and kissed her softly on her upper lip.

"Yes, I am lonely," Jessica replied, breathing heavily "and I
I want to be intimate with someone." She started caving in. It had
been a long time since a man kissed her like that.

"So, what is the problem?" Derrick kissed her ear.

"I feel like you are asking me to say yes to the devil," she pushed
him away from her ear, trembling. He was making her feel things
she hadn't felt for a very long time, but they were coming at a price.
Derrick reached for the diamond ring in his pocket and showed it
to her.

"I am saying, later tonight I will come over to your place. We are
going to make love and then you can plan the wedding of your
dreams. Or are we through? What's the verdict?"

Jessica sat there in silence. Temptation had never been so hard to
resist before. Derrick was offering her everything she had ever
wanted. She was wasting away, waiting for a dream that seemed
too far to reach. It was time to throw in the towel.

"I feel as if I have just sold my soul to the devil," she softly replied
in fear.

"Is that a yes?" he asked smiling.

Tears dripping down her face, she replied, "It's a yes."

Derrick placed the ring back in his pocket and embraced her. He spoke victoriously, "You will get the ring after we make love. You made the right decision."

To Jessica it felt like the wrong decision. She felt she had lost everything that kept her alive. She had lost her dream and it was so sad. She embraced him, closing her eyes and mouthing a little prayer, making sure he could not hear her.

"Oh God please forgive me and save me before it's too late."

Smugly, Derrick moved back to his seat, and they ate their dinner in relative silence. Jessica took a cab back home because he had things to do in town before their romantic night.

The Bar Fight

Adam found himself in Mike's bar. It was easier to drown himself inside a bottle instead of dealing with his problems. Even in his drunken state, he still looked like a regular Tom Cruise, handsome with dark brown hair, green eyes, a well chiselled body and a face fit for the screen.

"Hey man, why don't you go home to your beautiful wife?" said Mike, the barman and owner. Mike was a regular church going man. He didn't have the looks, but he had the heart. He was an average forty-three-year-old, blond, plump man with red freckles, and at this moment he had his gaze fixed upon Adam with a mixture of disgust and shame.

Adam

"Why don't you mind your own business?" Adam said with slurred speech. It was midnight and the pair were the only people left in the bar. He pulled out a slab of chocolate and started tearing the wrapping which was labelled *Destiny*. Eating chocolate whilst drinking was a strange quirk he had, which people often remarked on.

"Listen man, I happen to love *my* wife, so drink up and we can both go home," Mike sneered in a condescending tone. Adam was starting to get very agitated. He shoved the chocolate back in his pocket.

"What is that supposed to mean?" he looked straight at Mike.

"Figure it out man. The last thing I want to do is sit here nursing a drunk, cheating husband who feels sorry for himself," came the harsh retort.

Adam could feel the anger boiling up from the pit of his stomach. "You don't understand anything so just shut up!"

"I understand plenty! The *whole town* knows!" Mike shouted.

"It's not that easy, you self-righteous pig!" Adam shouted back at Mike. The screaming match became louder and louder.

"Sure, it is. You could try harder!"

"I can't!"

Chapter 1

"Yes, you can!"

Without any warning Adam suddenly pulled Mike over the counter and punched him in the face. Mike landed on the floor on his back. As he dazedly tried to sit up, he found Adam pinning him down with a barstool and could not get up.

"Get up!" Adam shouted doing his best to taunt him in the process.

"I can't; you have me trapped, stupid!" Mike shouted back at him.

"Come on try harder!"

Mike, tried as hard as he could to move the chair, but couldn't. The more he tried to push the chair off, the harder Adam pushed and leaned over it, keeping him pinned on the floor. Finally, he could not take it anymore.

"I can't!" Mike screamed.

"You can!" Adam screamed back. Silence fell and the point Adam was trying to prove dawned on Mike. "See it's not that easy!"

"Come on man, it's not the same" Mike replied defensively.

"It totally *is* the same!" Adam shouted in torment.

Mike went dumb. He finally understood how hard it was for Adam to stay faithful to his wife. Adam, satisfied that he had made his point, helped him up. Then he walked towards the door. As he reached it, he turned around. His rage had subsided, and, in its place, pain was written all over his face.

"Don't judge me, Mike. You don't know what the hell I am going through."

He walked away without looking back, missing the look of shame and guilt that swept across Mike's face for being so judgemental. "I don't know if you are real or not and I never asked you for anything in my whole life but if you can hear me, save me from the hell I am living in." Adam prayed as he walked down the street looking for his next conquest.

The Letter

Adam was surprised to find Sarah standing by the door, holding a letter. She could not contain her excitement but was hesitant to share it with her husband.

"You didn't come home yesterday and...." she said, following her husband from the door into the kitchen.

Adam did not allow her to finish the sentence. "It's not the first time I didn't sleep at home. So what's the problem?" he asked rudely, opening the fridge and reaching for a beer. Sarah placed the letter she was holding on the kitchen table and sat on the chair, waiting for him to turn around, but he didn't.

Chapter 1

Finally, she said, "We won a holiday." She said it calmly, trying very hard to contain her elation. Smiles were rarely seen in the Phillips family. Adam was surprised when he turned around and found one on his wife's face.

"I have been waiting to tell you about it," Sarah said. He liked the smile on her face and was surprised to find himself smiling too. Was it contagious or was it the good news he was hearing from his wife that was putting him in a good mood?

"What holiday are you talking about?" he asked sitting down next to her and putting the beer on the table.

"It seems you and I have been buying so many of those chocolates.... what's the name?" Sarah asked in a hurry.

"*Destiny*," Adam answered impatiently, eager for Sarah to carry on speaking.

"Yes, that's it!" she shrieked excitedly. "We have won a holiday on a yacht for seven days!"

"Wait, what?" He was trying to gather his thoughts.
Sarah could see the perplexed expression on his face.

"The letter says we have been such good customers because every month we buy a packet of this brand's chocolate. This is their way of thanking us," she slowly and calmly explained to her confused husband. Adam in disbelief, opened his beer and took a huge gulp. "I find all this so strange, Adam. How can they know when we buy them?"

"You have to fill a form every time you buy that particular chocolate. Maybe that's how."

"But why?"

"So that people like us can win a trip I guess." Adam was now more excited than she was. Without thinking, Sarah threw her arms around Adam's neck, but quickly removed them.
"Sorry Adam, I wasn't thinking, I am just so overjoyed," She hesitantly explained herself. Adam put his arms around her waist.
"It's alright I understand," it had been years since Adam touched her or could stand being touched by his wife, "so when are we leaving?"

"Tomorrow morning at five," Sarah said, "A limo is taking us to a private airport and then we fly out to some exotic island where a luxury yacht is waiting for us," unable to believe she was being touched by her husband. 'This is exactly what we need. If Adam can hold me just on hearing the news of the trip, imagine what it will do for our marriage when we get there!' she thought to herself. The feeling of his arm around her waist made her ecstatic, and she reciprocated by throwing hers around his neck and kissing him impulsively on the mouth. Adam suddenly felt very uncomfortable. The kiss felt like a blow from a hammer, and he needed to get away. He peeled himself from the embrace, muttering "I'm beat" as he cleared his throat. He walked to the lounge, threw himself on the couch and turned on the TV. "Uh....well you better start packing then, I'm going to doze off here, see you later."

The pain of being rejected was familiar. It was like the familiar scent of her favourite perfume she wore everyday which was a birthday gift from Adam; she accepted it with resignation just like the empty shell that was their marriage. Yet this time, there was a glimpse of hope in her eyes, as she happily started packing for the trip.

The Knock at the Door

James lay in his bed feeling disappointed and defeated. He felt physically and emotionally tired and had been unable to sleep since he found out about the pregnancy. He kept thinking about his conversation with her, starring straight up at the ceiling, unable to move an inch. He had no strength left; all the stuffing had been knocked out of him.

When he saw the sun rising from his bedroom, he realized that he had been up the whole night. James turned on his right side and opened his side drawer and took the slab of chocolate lying on the drawer. He lay on his back, eating the chocolate piece by piece. He looked at the wrapping cover all over and called out the name on the cover. "*Destiny* my foot!" James was interrupted from his morbid thoughts by a knock at the door.

"James are you up?" It was his father.

"Yeah, I am coming," James replied.

His father came in holding something in his hand. "This is for you". He was holding up a letter and threw it onto his son's bed. Reginald was a cold man with frigid contemptuous rust-coloured eyes, lines

above his dark stocky brow and a receding hairline. The age spots on his face and a neat salt and pepper beard indicated that he was sixty-year-old man.
He was a lean man with the same athletic body as his son but short in stature.

"Thanks," James replied.
He was finding it very uncomfortable to have his father in his room. Although they lived in the same house, both preferred never to be in each other's space. They lived separate lives. The only time they were in the same room was at the workplace. He and his father found it very difficult to construct a sentence that could lead them to having a conversation with each other.
"OK then, get ready for work," Reginald said and walked out. James opened the letter and was happy to discover that he had won a trip to an exotic island on a cruise ship, for seven days. This was exciting news! He had never won anything in his life! He thought to himself. He yelled in excitement, "Hell yeah!"

His father came running through the door saying: "Have you lost your damn mind! Why are you shouting like that?"

"I won Pop!" James cried in excitement. He could not contain the joy he was feeling.

"Won what? And stop that screaming!" Reginald shouted back. James was brought back from his euphoria to reality. "Sorry I didn't mean to disrespect you Sir," James apologetically replied. "I won a trip to an island for seven days."

Chapter 1

"What! Did you enter a competition?" his father asked in confusion.

"No sir, I won by buying this specific chocolate," James replied while taking out another slab of chocolate from the drawer and gave it to his father. "I have been buying so many of these chocolates that the company is thanking me by giving me a trip. You see, you have to fill a form each time you buy one and that's how they chose me."

"Does this mean you are going to miss work for seven days?" Reginald asked.

James was afraid to answer that question. Would his father keep him from going on this trip? Could his father be that cruel? He thought to himself. Hesitantly he finally answered, "Yes sir."

Reginald surprised the both of them with the words coming out of his mouth. "Fine, but I expect you to work extra hours when you come back."

James could not believe what he was hearing. His father had a heart after all, he thought to himself. Out of gratitude and excitement, he hugged him. "Thank you, sir, I will work long hours. You won't be disappointed."

"Alright James, he said clearing his throat. "I will see you when you come back," his father replied as he pulled away from his son and walked out of his room.

The Visit from Donna

Jessica was standing in front of the mirror naked, late in the evening. This was the night she was going to give her chastity away to a man she knew, deep inside, she didn't love. She had compromised on something which she had vowed never to do. She had been determined to be different and had promised herself to never get married for the sake of it... She had waited for love, believing she would have the night she had dreamed of and imagined for many years. The night she would find someone who truly deserved her. To be loved with her imperfections and for her soul, not for her body or the inheritance left by her parents who had died in a car crash. Instead, cupid played a sadistic joke of bringing fake marriage proposals from married heart breakers or money-hungry philanderers who only wanted one thing; to sleep with her, fleeing as soon as they figured out they weren't going to succeed. It was never for love. Jessica neatly packed her broken heart away, each time they revealed their true colours. She prayed to God that the next time she fell in love it would last forever.

She tried to keep herself fit but she could not fight time. The years had played a cruel joke on Jessica. Her body was starting to look like a flat tyre. She squeezed her flabby stomach with its love handles, whilst looking at herself in the mirror. Jessica turned around as she touched her loose thighs. It seemed that her thighs were determined to get bigger in spite of her exercise regime. She kept turning around looking at her body. Time to stop looking at mirrors! Derrick is going to take one look at me and run for the hills! She said, thinking out loud.

Chapter 1

"No, he won't. Not when I am done with you," she heard someone saying.

Startled by the fact that she was not alone yet she was completely naked, Jessica grabbed the towel on the dressing table and turned around to see who had come into her house unannounced. She was relieved to see her best friend, Donna, staring at her with a smile on her face. Donna had let herself in and come to the bedroom. "Your door is unlocked. Did you know that?" she strolled towards her, amused. Her chubby, well-shaped curves, large bust and broad hips manifested her confident and exuberant nature. Blessed with thick lips, lush eyelashes and a narrow pointy nose, her eyes sparkled brightly, matching the colourful air of her red braids. The vivacious thirty-three-year-old, lived life on her own terms.

"I do now," Jessica replied with a laugh. "What are you doing here?" Jessica asked.

"A little birdie told me that someone is doing the deed with Derrick tonight and I am offering you my services free of charge to make you look fabulous.," Donna replied as she threw her bright lime green handbag on the bed.

"How could you know that!" Jessica asked, dumbfounded by what she was hearing. "Ah let me guess," Jessica continued without waiting to hear what Donna had to say. "Derrick told you!" she screamed out.

Adam

"Please don't be angry with him or me, until you hear me out," Donna pleaded while sitting at the dressing table.

"I am listening," Jessica responded furiously, folding her arms.

"I didn't just set you up with Derrick. We have been discussing, ways to gently persuade you, to go all the way with him!" Donna said guardedly, with a tinge of fear.

"You have been feeding him information about me!" Jessica replied furiously. "That's why he knew so much at the restaurant! Of all the appalling things you could do to me, this is the worst! Some friend you are! You and Derrick have been manipulating me from the start!" she said staring at her best friend with accusing eyes.
"I was trying to help you." Tears started to fall from Donna's eyes. She could not stand to see Jessica so angry with her.

"Yeah right! How could you possibly think this is helping me!" Jessica shouted back at Donna.

The altercation between them finally got the best of Donna. Out of pain and frustration she blurted out, "What was I supposed to do, watch my best friend remain alone because of her beliefs!" She carried on without taking a breath, "How could I allow a beautiful woman with a good heart, who deserves so much love and happiness remain miserable!" Jessica was speechless, as she watched her friend wipe her tears from her eyes. "I know you Jessica". The fight was exhausting Donna. She could not shout anymore. "If it is not on your terms, you split! So, Derrick played along enough to keep you interested."

Finally, Jessica managed to form a sentence after her long silence. "I feel so humiliated. I am calling Derrick and cancelling." She started to walk towards her cell phone on the bedside table.

"No, you can't do that!" Donna said, blocking her trying to keep her from reaching it. Jessica started to lose her patience.

"Get out of my way Donna!"

"Remember Caleb," Donna said with accusation in her eyes.

Tears fell down Jessica's cheeks. "Why are you bringing that up?" she responded hurt.
"Because I am not going to let you make the same mistake you did with him," Donna said.

"That was different," Jessica replied defensively.

"Oh really? You did not realize what you had with him!" Donna said bluntly.

It was very difficult for Jessica to talk about Caleb. She was nineteen when they got involved. He had been nothing but a gentleman. Sweet and loving towards her, loving her for who she was and not for how she looked or what she owned. Unfortunately for him, she was still besotted with Kevin, who was nothing but a womaniser and only appeared back in her life when Caleb was in the picture. Stupidly, Jessica accepted Kevin back into her heart. Kevin then did what came naturally to him; he hurt her and walked out of her life again as soon as Caleb was out of the picture. Jessica felt as if someone had slapped her on the face as she started reliving the whole thing in her mind. She walked back to the bed and sat there in silence.

"First love is nothing but a curse," Donna sympathetically continued. Feeling sorry for Jessica, Donna sat next to her and didn't say anything more.

"Caleb promised to marry me," Jessica said with a heavy heart. "I didn't know that blessings could be missed in the blink of an eye until him. I didn't know Donna I really thought Kevin was the one. How could I know anything about love when I didn't love myself? Having a relationship with God taught me to love myself and I discovered the kind of love and man I deserved. If I had known God earlier, I would have known these things and chosen the wonderful man Caleb is, instead of that fool Kevin." It was as if Jessica was trying to defend her actions to Donna.

"But by that time, it was too late," Donna said sympathetically.

"No, I still had time, but my guilt did allow me to go after him. I didn't believe I deserved a second chance after I had hurt him that way."

Chapter 1

"By the time you realized you did, he was gone, married to someone else."

"Why did I lose Caleb?" Jessica cried out. She could not stop the tears from falling over and over again from her eyes. Donna took a piece of tissue from the tissue box lying on the bedside table and started to wipe Jessica's face.

"Why did I have to lose Caleb, Donna?" Jessica asked, as she finally managed to stop crying.

"You were so concerned with that mumbo jumbo you see in the movies, it was all about the love you were feeling instead of how Kevin treated you," Donna replied. "What if Derrick is your second chance?" she continued. "Maybe you can learn to love him in time." Jessica started to cry all over again. "Jess, you think life is a fairy tale but it's not. It's hard and cruel. It's about compromising, to get what you want. I did it and I got what I wanted. It's about the survival of the fittest, Eat or be eaten." Donna was convincing.
"You don't have to tell me that. I know life is not fair. I did not get a second chance with Caleb. I lost him," Jessica sadly replied.

"Then *pleeease*, don't make the same mistake with Derrick." It was an impassioned plea.
"If I could turn back time, I would be with Caleb, instead of settling with Derrick," Jessica replied painfully. "Losing Caleb has left me with nothing but regret."

"It's excruciating to love someone you can never have Jessica," Donna said, sympathetically. Jessica kept silent; some things were hard for her to admit or say out loud. "If you had a second chance, would you settle for Caleb?" Donna asked.

"It would never be settling if it was Caleb but lightning doesn't strike the same place twice," Jessica said with teary smile.

"So, am I forgiven?" Donna asked with loving eyes.

"I know you had my best interests at heart, but why did you have to go to such desperate measures?"

"Because you are a desperate case!" Donna teased.

"Ha-ha!" Jessica replied. She sighed as she laughed. Soft, fresh tears started streaming down her face.

"Come on let's get you ready for tonight, Derrick will be here soon," Donna said, trying to cheer Jessica up. She was the owner of a well-established hairdressing salon in town. "Let's see, we are going to need make up and..." But the phone rang and stopped Donna from finishing her sentence. It was Derrick.

"Hello," Jessica said, as she answered her cell phone.

"It's me. I can't make it tonight."

"Oh" Jessica said dumbfounded.

35

Chapter 1

"I am in the hospital," he said plainly. "I was rushing to get there, and I lost control of the car, and I hit a tree in the process."

"What! Are you OK?" she asked in concern.

"I broke my leg, but I am fine, I am going to be here for a couple of days."

Jessica could not help the smile forming on her face when Derrick said that.

"I will come and see you tomorrow." she put a loving tone into it.

"Ok but I am so upset about tonight." He was audibly upset and the irony of throwing a tantrum at her over his own reckless driving was not lost on Jessica.
She made mental excuses for him, pinning it down to the pain and shock; "It's OK Derrick, you just concentrate on getting better. I'll see you tomorrow."
"OK goodnight," he said and cut the call abruptly.

Jessica lingered on the dropped connection momentarily, struck by his coldness. "Derrick is in hospital," she told Donna as she hung up. Donna was startled and wanted to hear about it. "He hit a tree and broke his leg. I am going to see him tomorrow."

"What!" Donna said in concerned shock. "I am coming with you." Derrick was a very good friend of her husband Mike the bar owner and herself. "Well, since my skills are no longer needed I am going home to my man, it's been an emotional day". Donna said standing up from the bed.

"Thank you for everything," Jessica said.

"So, Miss Jessica Washington did I get through to you," Donna asked with a smile.

"Trust me I am not making the same mistake again," Jessica said adamantly.

"I know you won't. You know better now," Donna said as she quickly winked at Jessica and walked out of the room.

Alone in her room once again, Jessica checked on her mail and opened the envelope in a gold wrapping paper. The words "*Destiny*" were written on top. She read the letter. She was thrilled to discover she had won a trip to an exotic island on a cruise ship for seven days! Apparently buying her favourite chocolate named *Destiny* so often, had won her the trip. She was so happy that her bathrobe fell onto the floor as she started dancing around her bedroom completely naked.

Chapter 1

Chapter 2

The Plane Ride

J ames was the first to board the plane. It was a private Lear Jet with comfortable executive seating for 8 passengers. He was wondering if he was going to be the only African American on the trip when to his relief, Jessica Washington, the schoolteacher from town, stepped out of a limo next to the private plane. He waited for her to board and sit down. When James saw that Jessica was comfortable, he leaned across the aisle and greeted her. "It's nice to see a familiar face on this plane," James said in a friendly voice.

"Hi, you're James Franklyn from the vet," Jessica lifted her hand to shake James' hand.

"Guilty as charged," James said as he took it.

"Oh, my goodness you won too," Jessica replied happily. "I am so relieved to have someone I know on this trip, someone from the same community". Jessica said.
"We don't know each other that well," James teased.

"Well, I know *about* you, living in a small place and all. You know what I mean," She replied, laughing.
"Yeah, I know. The curse of living in a small town; everybody knows everybody." He joked. Jessica laughed out loud. They started making small talk.

"Why don't we sit together?" James said.

"Oh!" Jessica said feeling awkward by his' offer.

"I mean I am not coming on to you or anything. I just thought, since we are both alone, I could be your big brother and we could have fun together. I am sorry, did I step out of line?" James asked.

"It's alright James. I know you are involved with somebody. The curse of a small town and all," Jessica said repeating his exact words. He nodded shyly. "You look too young to be a big brother," she teased.

"Well, I am twenty-seven!" James shot back proudly.

"I am thirty-one and I would love to have a little brother and friend," She said with a smile. James looked at her and could not help grinning. He had never been so comfortable talking to someone of the opposite sex before. She had a calming effect on him.
"We can watch over each other's back," Jessica said in a warm tone.

"That's' exactly what I was thinking," He said as he sat next to her.

"You don't look thirty-one"
"Thanks I've got great gins" She played along

Adam and Sarah boarded the plane. "Wow, James from the vet and Jessica, the schoolteacher, are both here," Adam said to his wife out of surprise.
James overheard what he was saying and motioned with his hand that they should join them. The couple walked toward them and took the seats beside them.

"Isn't this crazy? Four people from the same town win the same trip, at the same time!" James said with excitement as he shook the couple's hands.

"I know," Sarah said with a shy smile.
"Mr and Mrs Phillips, it's so good to have the two of you here," Jessica said.
Before the couple could answer, the air hostess informed everybody to fasten their seat belts. The plane was getting ready

for take-off. Everybody was very excited to be going on this trip. You could hear the anticipation in their voices and feel the electric atmosphere. They were happy to escape their lives, even if it was just for a little while.

"Jessica, I am so glad you are here. Maybe we could get to know each other better," Sarah said shyly.

"I would like that," Jessica said. "I have always seen you in church but I just never had the chance to speak to you."

Sarah nodded and said, "I have felt that way too."
Adam gave Jessica a smile and said, "I hope we can get to know each other too."

"Definitely," Jessica replied suspiciously unsure of his motive and what was hidden behind that smile.

Adam could tell from her reply that Jessica knew about his infamous reputation. He quickly started a conversation with James while Sarah pretended she didn't see what had just transpired.
Adam said, "James, I hardly ever see you in town or at the bar."

"I know, my dad keeps me busy at work," James replied regretfully.

Maybe we can rectify that situation on this trip," Adam said.

"You bet!" James responded.

At that moment, the air hostess brought glasses of champagne. "Hey, let's make a toast!" James said with excitement, as everybody reached for their glasses and lifted them into the air. "To the best trip of our lives. May it be everything we wished for and more!" James exclaimed. Everybody clinked their glasses and cheered in joy. me?"

"Cheers!" they all said.

"Excuse me for a minute, I have to make a call," Jessica said, standing up. James stood up from his seat and allowed her to pass. A thought had suddenly come to Jessica's mind. She went to a seat out of earshot and picked up the phone attached to the wall by the window seat. She started dreading the conversation she was going to have. It was Derrick she needed to call. His cell phone started ringing and instantly, Derrick answered it.

"Hello Derrick," she said timidly.
"Where are you? I have been calling and calling!" Jessica started trembling. She went blank and silent. "Jessica!" Derrick screamed out furiously. The scream brought her back to her senses.

"On a plane," Jessica said in a soft voice, almost a whisper.

"You are where?" Derrick furiously asked. He was livid.

"I discovered last night that I had won a trip when I opened my mail. I am sorry," She quickly tried to appease the situation.

"Why didn't you call me after reading that stupid letter!"

"It didn't occur to me. I was so excited; I wasn't thinking straight. Please forgive me,"
Tears started to appear in her eyes. There was a side of Derrick that scared her. He made her feel like a child. "I am so sorry Derrick. I was so excited, if it's any consolation I didn't call Donna too," she said in a little girl's voice.
"I know, she was here. Apparently, you were supposed to come together. She has been calling you too,"

"Please don't be angry. I just had to go. I, I...," she hesitated, "I needed to go," Jessica desperately said, pleading for his forgiveness. Derrick took a deep a breath. It was how he calmed himself down.

"If you wanted me to take you on a trip you could have said so. "I feel like you are running away," He said accusingly, trying to keep his anger from rising up again.

"No, never!" Jessica said in a little voice, trying to hide the guilt in it. "Our plans were interrupted by your accident," She said.

"Maybe you are glad that they were," he blatantly replied. "Maybe we should call this whole thing off! This relationship is a joke and I have just had enough," he said spitefully.

"No Derrick please don't," she begged. "This trip is my way of saying goodbye to whom I have been for years, I really need this. I can't explain it, but I promise you when I get back, I will do anything you want me to do. Anything." She pleaded in desperation.

Chapter 2

Tears poured down her face. Derrick was satisfied. He had made her beg. It was never his intention to break up with her. He just needed her to remember he was in control.

"Remember you need me more than I do you," he said, out of spite.
"I know, I am so sorry Derrick," Jessica said. The tears kept falling one after another. A part of her didn't want to have anything to do with him or his ultimatums, but she felt he was her only chance for a normal life. Derrick could hear the desperation in her voice.

"Fine," he said. "Call me when you land," he demanded.
"I left my phone. We were instructed not to bring any phones, so that we don't have any distractions," She fearfully replied. His anger started to well up again. Derrick was very manipulative.

"I am very angry with you right now and very disappointed in you Jessica," he said. Jessica started feeling weak in the knees; she was being scolded like a little girl.

"It will never happen again," Jessica said in a small broken voice. Derrick had made his point. "I can be Mr nice guy again, he thought to himself.

"If this trip will help you forget all this nonsense of keeping yourself until marriage. Then I am all for it," he said.

"Thank you, Derrick. I promise you this is the last time I am going to disappoint you," she said out of relief.

"I am losing my patience with you. It had better be the last time, Jessica. You are not the only pebble on the shore. Do you hear me?"

"Loud and clear," Jessica managed to say. She was deeply hurt. Derrick knew just what to say to make her feel small.

"Bye, see you when you come back," He smugly replied and dropped the phone before she could answer.

"Bye," Jessica replied to a beeping phone. She placed the phone on the wall and cried, out of humiliation and confusion. Why did Derrick have to be so mean when he was angry? What kind of life would she be subjecting herself to? She thought to herself, with fresh tears wetting her cheeks.

James was still having a good time chatting with Sarah, and Adam and drinking champagne when they heard someone crying. They turned and realized it was Jessica.

"Excuse me guys but I am going to see what's going on," James said.

"Listen man," Adam said. "Me and the Mrs are going to get some shut eye. Had to wake up early this morning, the limo picked us up at five today," Adam said as he yawned.

"Same here," James replied. "You two catch up on your sleep."

"So, we will talk to Jessica later," Adam said while taking a pillow.

"I would come with you, but I am afraid I would not be much help right now," Sarah said. "I didn't realize I was so tired," she continued, while taking the pillow from Adam's hand and placing it behind his head.

"Thanks," Adam said in a whisper. It was always uncomfortable for Adam when Sarah touched him. Sarah noticed how uncomfortable he was feeling; she pretended not to be hurt by it.

"So, James you will apologize for the both of us," she said.

"I am sure she will understand," James said as he walked away. He sensed the tension between the couple and guessed it was because of Adam's cheating. Everyone in town knew about Adam. But right now, Jessica was his main concern, he thought to himself as he walked down the aisle towards Jessica and sat beside her. "Is everything alright?" he asked out of concern.

"Yes, I am fine," Jessica said as she quickly wiped her tears with a tissue. Her face looked flushed, and she had red eyes.

"Look, it's none of my business, but I can see you're upset, and I want to help if I can," he said as he took the tissue and wiped a new tear appearing from her eye. "I am your brother on this trip after all," James said with a smile.

Jessica was touched that he cared." OK bro." She breathed in deeply and exhaled slowly as she started telling James the reason for her tears. "My boyfriend is angry at me because I went on this trip while he is in hospital."

"Why didn't you tell him?"

"There is more," Jessica said looking intently at him. James listened in silence.
"He wants to marry me."

"Wow that's great news," James said excitedly.

"There is more," Jessica said in frustration.

James realized he needed to keep quiet and stop interrupting her when she was speaking. "I am sorry, I am listening," he said.

"Derrick wants to sleep with me before we get married and I have always wanted my wedding night to be the night I give myself to someone," Jessica said. She looked at him straight in the eye to see if he would judge her too.

"You have never been with someone?" James asked awkwardly. He could not believe he was actually having this discussion with a woman in the twenty first century.
 "I know you think this is stupid," Jessica said exasperated. She could judge from James's reaction that he didn't understand where she was coming from.

"No, no, I don't think it's stupid, it's your dream," he said as he put his hand on her shoulder. Jessica could not believe what she was hearing. It was a response she was not expecting from a man.

"You understand?" She asked in disbelief.

James nodded. "I always wanted to be a musician, but instead I am getting married to a woman I feel nothing for because she is pregnant with my baby. So yes, I understand perfectly," he said. Jessica was grateful to find someone on her side. She had never met any man like James. So open-minded, Jessica thought to herself.

James laid his hand on the back of his head as he stretched backwards on the seat and closed his eyes. "I need to think about what I am leaving behind. This trip will help me get to terms with the fact that once I marry Melanie, there is no chance of my dream ever coming true."

Jessica lay back and closed her eyes as she said, "If I sleep with Derrick my dream will be gone forever. I keep wondering if this is what I have been waiting for all my life. What is this life all about? Could Derrick be the silver lining?"

They were both silent for a while, lost in thought.

James started to sing softly, "Is this love that I am feeling? Could this be love that I have been searching for?"

"I love that song, it is by White snake," Jessica said.

"Every time I hear that song it's as if the artist is experiencing a love he has always wanted and cannot believe that he finally has received," James said emotionally.

"That's how I feel too," Jessica said softly. They both shared a sigh at the same time, and both laughed at the realization. "James your voice is so beautiful," Jessica said sincerely.

"Thank you, my mother sang in the choir, she had the voice of an angel," He said reliving her memory in his mind.

"Had?" Jessica asked as she turned and looked at James, afraid of what she was going to hear.

James opened his eyes, looking up he said, "Cancer." It took everything for him not to cry.

"I am so sorry," Jessica said. She could feel the pain he was trying to hide.
"I was thirteen when it happened," James said, closing his eyes to prevent a tear from falling down his cheek. "Singing has never been allowed in the Franklyn house since she's been gone." James had never opened up to anyone like this before. He was thankful to have someone to listen to him for a change.

"You would have been a great artist James,"

"Thanks," James said with a smile. Jessica turned and closed her eyes again. Silence became their means of conversation.

51

Finally, she broke the silence and said, "I think it's time to grow up James, for the both of us."

"I am afraid you're right," James said. There was nothing left to be said. The friendship they just found did not find words necessary. Jessica felt safe around James, it was as if she had known him all her life. In silence they drifted back to their thoughts. It had been a long day. Emotionally and physically, James and Jessica were exhausted. They drifted to sleep, both thinking about what might have been if their dreams had come true.

The Accusation

Sarah woke up and found Adam watching her. She was surprised but happy at the thought of being watched while sleeping by her husband. "Hey," she said as she rubbed her eyes. "What time is it?" she was still drowsy.

"Don't know, but its dark outside, look," Adam said as he gestured Sarah to look at the window with his head. Sarah looked out from her window seat and realized it was pitch black outside. She was shocked.

"We could not have possibly slept the whole day, that's impossible!" Sarah exclaimed. She could not believe she had spent so much time sleeping. "I mean I don't sleep that long even at home," she said looking at Adam for an answer.

"Relax," Adam said laughingly, seeing how disturbed she was about the whole situation. "Maybe we just needed to relax more than we thought."

Sarah realized that Adam was making sense and decided not to take the whole thing so seriously. "I guess," she said getting up.

"Where are you going?" Adam asked.
"To see Jessica," She replied.

"They are sleeping, I checked." Sarah leaned from her chair and looked down the aisle. She saw that James and Jessica were sound asleep. She sat back on her seat.

"They didn't move back to their seats. I wonder why she was so upset this morning,"

"Don't know and don't care," Adam said arrogantly.

"Adam!" Sarah said in a reproaching tone.

"What!" Adam asked indignantly. Sarah could see from Adam's reaction that he was angry she had scolded him.

"Nothing," She said quietly. "You just sound so insensitive that's all."

"I just want to relax on this trip. We are supposed to take it easy, leaving everything behind, even if it's just for a little while. That's what she is supposed to do," Adam said pointing down the aisle with his finger.

"I guess you're right," Sarah replied. She didn't agree with what he was saying, but decided it was best not to say anything.

"I am glad they are sleeping,"

"Why?"

"I want us to talk," Adam calmed down. A big smile appeared on Sarah's face. Her husband never wanted to talk. Maybe this trip was working wonders already, she thought to herself.

"OK," she said sitting up and looking at him.

"I feel different being here with you somehow," Adam said. He sat up straight and looked at Sarah.

"Me too," Sarah replied with a smile. These are exactly the words she wanted to hear coming out of her husband's mouth, she thought to herself touching his hands.

"But," Adam said, as he slowly pulled his hands away from hers. The expression on Sarah's face changed and Adam noticed.

"I don't want you to have any expectations of me." He looked straight into her eyes. He wanted Sarah to hear exactly what he was saying. "We both know the reality of our situation. So, let's not pretend, OK." He looked serious.

"Oh," Sarah said. She was hurt and she could not hide the pain from her eyes. "I thought this trip will bring us closer. I am sorry I guess I was wrong."

Adam looked down for a while before looking up again. "The last thing I ever want to do is hurt you, but it's all I ever seem to do," Adam said feeling lost. "So please Sarah, don't make it so easy for me," Adam said in desperation.

"I don't understand," Sarah replied in confusion.

"No touching," Adam said accusingly.

Sarah nodded her head with a broken heart and kept back the tears that were attempting to fall from her face with a smile. Sarah wanted her husband happy, even if it was at her expense. She knew being distant was out of his control. The least she could do was to be understanding, she thought to herself. "All I want Adam, is to make things easy for you and I want you to enjoy yourself on this trip. So, I promise you. No more touching," she said jokingly. He laughed and reached out to touch his wife's chin but stopped himself before reaching it.

"Thanks for being such a trooper about all of this," he said, relieved.

Chapter 2

"Hey that's me, a trooper what can I say," Sarah said while smiling with understanding eyes.

"Listen I am starving," Adam said. "I am going to and see what I can get to eat. Can I order you anything?"

"You decide," she answered.

He gave Sarah a smile as he got up to speak to the air hostess. When Sarah was left alone, she allowed the tears she was holding back to fall. She consoled herself by thinking, it's better to have a little of her husband instead of not having him at all. Adam came back to find her sleeping. He smiled as he looked at her. He was so glad that Sarah was handling this situation so maturely. Their relationship may not be easy, but it worked for them. They were coping, Adam thought to himself. By the time the air hostess came back with mashed potatoes, peas and a nice juicy steak, he was asleep. The air hostess laughed and went away with the food. The four passengers slept soundly and were suddenly awakened the next morning, by the sound of the plane landing.

Chapter 3

The Island

Beholding the endless bright green and blue island for the first time was truly a magical sight to see, with the enchanting palm trees swaying in the soft breeze and sparkling blue water. The smell of the tall coconut, mango, and pineapple trees mingled together, creating an exotic island cocktail for the senses. The flowers turned the island into a colourful purple, red, pink and yellow canvass, and the island was surrounded by majestic mountains. The exotic breath-taking scenery made the enthralled group gasp at the beauty of their surroundings.

The four vacationers had no recollection of how they arrived at the island as they all stood on the white sandy beach. The last memory they all had was sleeping on the air plane but that didn't seem to matter as they gazed at the beauty that was surrounding them. A speedboat was waiting for them in the most picturesque ocean they had ever seen. Everybody climbed in and they were greeted by the Caribbean boat pilot. He steered in silence, allowing his guests to be mesmerized by the serene beauty of the island. The deep turquoise-blue water stretched out as far as the eye could see, seemingly infinite. The speedboat came closer and closer to a luxury super-yacht floating in the middle of the ocean. They were struck by its awesome beauty from afar; its enormity took their breath away.

The travellers were met by four Caribbean crew members, two men and two women who announced that they would be at their beck and call, welcoming them aboard their beautiful super-yacht called "*Believe*" with glasses of champagne. The women wore golden turbans and white dashikis with golden embroidered detail on the collar, cuffs and down the front.

A dark Caribbean man in his fifties greeted them in Creole, "Hello, my name is Anton. May I show you around the yacht?" He wore a white dashiki made of the same fabric with the same embroidered detail as the others. Anton had dark inviting eyes, a clean cut but bushy Howard Moon moustache and bare smooth head. He had a smile hidden in the corner of his mouth ready to break through in all its fullness and brightness. He was a well bodied man compared to his age. His glowing dark brown skin confirmed the many years he had been kissed by the sun rays.

"Yes, you may," Jessica smiled warmly.

Chapter 3

"Follow me please."

They trooped after Anton around the yacht. *Believe* had four decks, all accessible by a lift, taking them from one to the next. The yacht provided an aura of luxury with the extravagantly decorated Rococo furniture from the 18th century France period.

The lower deck was dedicated to fitness, with an on board gym and all sorts of water sport equipment. Fitness coaching was available, including Taebo and Karate lessons. Next to the gym, there was a games area filled with all the current versions of PlayStation, Xbox and Nintendo, including a pool table. Latin, Salsa and Meringue dance classes were also on offer for their enjoyment.

The first deck was dedicated to beauty, with a parlour where the ladies were given manicures and pedicures. On the same deck there was a massage room complete with a very large Jacuzzi and a pool for the girls and the men to enjoy. The second deck had a ladies boutique and an exclusive men's store where they could pick and choose all manner of clothing items and jewellery to wear during their vacation. It was a piece of heaven! The exhilaration and joy they all felt kept building in strength every time they went into a new area. The vast dining area was on the third deck and had three separate restaurants that offered different dishes from different countries including a bar. The dining area turned into an entertaining area during the night. A silver glittering ball and lights came down at the touch of a switch, creating a dance club atmosphere of lights and music. It was incredible!

"Tonight, we are going dancing!" James said as he took Sarah by the arm and waltzed with her. Adam followed suit and swept Jessica into his arms spinning her around as he lifted her into the air. The four passengers were thrilled; a lot of screaming came from Jessica and Sarah out of joy.

"Excuse me," Anton said in his deep Creole accent. His baritone voice instantly swept you into the tropical Caribbean Island spirit, "May I show you to your sleeping quarters?" The four of them practically ran after him like little kids full of
Innocence as he showed them to their rooms, which were on the lower deck, opposite the gym area. They all forgot themselves and their carefree laughter filled the entire passage.

Each cabin had personalized name plates affixed to the doors. Anton stood next to Adam and Sarah's cabin and handed Adam the room key. Adam entered the suite with Sarah, James and Jessica following. All of their mouths fell open as they surveyed the cabin. The master suite had an en suite bathroom with a Jacuzzi-styled bath and shower. It had an adjoining dressing room and an office. The upholstered wall covered the room with gold and silver floral designs. The pattern on the wall matched the carved decorations on the furniture including the sumptuous French bed that displayed the intricately carved wooden floral design around the curved legs and framing the delicately styled headboard.
The first- class bedroom was lavish, regal, and had ample space to walk around.

"Oh, my goodness!" Jessica cried.

"I feel as if I am in a palace," Sarah also remarked in awe.

Adam ran to the bathroom and could not believe what he saw "James you've got to see this, man!"
A second later James was standing right next to him. "A bath and a shower, dude, in silver and gold!" he exclaimed. "I have to see how my room looks like!"

James' cabin was adjacent to Adam and Sarah's'. The door was opened and Anton was patiently waiting for him inside. He handed James the keys to the room and politely walked out. When Adam, Sarah and Jessica heard James' whistling from his space, they all went to his room.

"Wow James your room is fit for a king," Sarah said as she entered. Everything in James' cabin was the same except for the colour of the upholstered floral wall and drapes, which were in gold including the bath and shower. The group looked around James' cabin, marvelling at its beauty.

Jessica spoke, "It's beautiful James!"

"The golden room!" Adam remarked in awe, as he sat on the Rococo sofa.

"I guess it's your turn Jessica," Sarah said as she took Jessica by the hand and led her to her cabin.

The Island

Anton was waiting outside Jessica's sleeping quarters, with the door opened. She and James were neighbours. "You're key Miss," he said as he handed it over.

"It's incredible!" Jessica marvelled, walking in.

"This is called the silver cabin," Anton announced, stepping in with Sarah.
"It should be called the Princess cabin," Sarah said, as she looked around, her breath taken away by the beauty of the space. Adam and James came in.

"What a room!" Adam whistled in wonder.

"Sparkling silver," James mused as he touched the drapes. The theme in Jessica's sleeping compartment was sparkling silver.

"It feels like I'm in an enchanted fairy tale," Jessica said as she looked around her, unable to stop giggling from the euphoria. It had the same French furniture as the other cabins' except the upholstered floral walls, drapes, bath and shower were in sparkling silver. Nobody could wipe away the beaming smile on Jessica's face. She was in love with it.

"Dinner will be served in the dining area at seven," Anton graciously announced as he went away.

"Is this really happening? Are we here and living in the most incredible rooms you have ever seen?" James wondered with reverence. "I mean guys; we are literally the only four passengers here on a massive luxury yacht. It's almost surreal, our own private piece of paradise for the next few days!"

"You took the words out of my mouth James, it's like some kind of fantasy. I feel like I'm in a dream or some kind of alternate universe but boy am I thrilled to be here!" Sarah agreed.

"To the island!" Adam mimicked a wrestling commentator and sent everyone into stitches. He pulled everybody into a tight bear hug. Meanwhile, outside, the water caressed the yacht's keel and bore it quietly out to the sea like a plotting supernatural force or mystic being.

James' Encounter

James lay in his king size bed in the golden room, looking up at the ceiling and thinking about the fun he and the gang had enjoyed that night. Dinner had been incredible; the chef had prepared a five-star cuisine with an enticing selection of gourmet dishes. He started laughing as he remembered Jessica fulfilling one of her bucket list's wishes, eating lobster. Reliving the night in his mind, he saw them seated at a round table. Sarah was having gourmet fish with stuffed cheese and spinach. Adam was wolfing down his oysters served with octopus.
In amused disbelief, he asked, "Adam, are you really that crazy that you could eat an octopus?"

"Hey man, you only live once," came the reply with a chuckle. "I am on holiday." He smiled at Jessica eating her lobster.

Jessica gave Adam a look that said she understood where he was coming from. She nodded and looked around the people at the table, "I've always wanted to eat lobster since I watched this big guy eating it on TV when I was five. He was a hero fighting for anyone who was being oppressed."

"I think I remember that movie," Sarah said with a gleam of light in her eyes laughing out loud from the memory. "He loved to eat and drink. What was his name?" Sarah asked with a giggle. Jessica nodded rapidly in agreement.

"Wait a minute I think I remember that movie," James cut in good-humouredly. "I think his nickname was Big Justice. It was a white guy with long curly hair and a moustache. I just can't remember for the life of me, his real name, or the movie he acted in."

"Wow! I'm surrounded by an old peoples Bingo group; none of you can remember the guy's name!" Adam yelled with mock indignation, teasing his friends.

Sarah threw a serviette that landed on her husband's face. "Shut up and eat your octopus."

Adam removed the serviette with a chuckle and loudly feigned shock, "Hey I am just shocked that I am surrounded by people whose memory has been affected by old age!"

"Who are you are calling old, Adam?" James yelled out, with a grin on his face. He threw down the gauntlet; "We will see who is old when we are on the dance floor at the club tonight. I'm going to be the last one leaving the floor."

The challenge was eagerly accepted, "Oh we will see about that James."

Jessica, who was ready for the dare, looked at James with a twinkle in her eye and said, "You are not the only one with moves you know."

"I think I better finish my ostrich," James feigned fear of his 'big sister' Jessica. He took a big bite of his fillet, smiling in amusement.

Adam went on the offensive, "Hey man, you are eating *ostrich* and you are teasing *me?*"

"It's better than octopus!" James countered in a loud voice, wincing at the octopus on Adam's plate.

"Honey, James is definitely right, anything is better than octopus!" Sarah added in stitches.

"I concur," Jessica joined the banter. Everybody was laughing at Adam's interesting choice of dish including Adam himself.

After dinner they went to the club and danced under the electric rainbow lights. They were having the time of their lives. Sarah and Jessica laughed at the two men trying to out-dance each other. James and Adam kept exchanging their partners. One moment

Adam would be dancing with Sarah, then suddenly out of the blue, he would hand her to James and dance with Jessica. Sometimes the two ladies would dance with each other laughing at the two men forced to dance
with one another. It was a sight to see! It had been a fun night. It was as if they had been friends for years. Surprisingly, the winner on the dance floor was Sarah. She was the last to leave, so full of energy, all her inhibitions completely gone!

"Everybody! Let's give Sarah a round of applause. The dance maniac!" James said in a loud wrestling announcer's voice. It was after midnight when everybody retired to their rooms.

James chuckled to himself as he replayed the night in his mind. He finally threw the covers off and decided to take a walk. He could not sleep, and figured it was out of excitement. But the truth was that he felt something was calling out to him. Encouraging him to leave his cabin at that particular time, at twelve midnight. His stroll brought him out into the dead of night and onto the open top deck of the ship. He peered down into the ocean as he held on to the railings.
Suddenly he heard someone calling his name in a whisper, "James..." Startled, he looked around to check if he wasn't alone, but was surprised to find that he was. He started feeling uneasy.

"James..."

'There it is again,' he thought to himself. 'Who could be up at this time of night and why won't they show themselves?'

"James..." This was the third time he heard something calling him in a hushed tone.

"Whoever you are show yourself right now!" he yelled into the night, betraying the false bravado, he was putting up.
He tried to calm himself down by looking at the sea.

"James." This time the murmur was coming from the dark waters. James felt drawn to it. He leaned gradually further over the railing, each time he heard his name being whispered. Suddenly a strong force grabbed him, pulling him over the railing and straight into the ocean. James could not believe what was happening to him.

He was being pulled speedily, with great intensity deeper and deeper to the bottom of the ocean. The first thought that came to his mind was, *I am going to die!* Before he could think about anything else, he had reached the bottom and was still alive, breathing under water! How could that be? And how was he able to walk under water? Terror permeated every fibre of his body. As if someone or something was reading his mind, he was suddenly surrounded by "a peace that he could not fathom." He felt calm and safe, marvelling at the beauty of the sea plants and the fish all around him. He was surprised that not one single fish tried to attack him. In fact, he felt welcomed by everything in the water.
James looked at his feet and was drawn to a small wooden birdhouse, slightly covered by sand. He bent down and picked it up. As he looked at it, he could not believe it was still intact. It looked weathered and worn down. 'It must have been here for years,' James thought to himself. He felt drawn to this birdhouse. Turning

it around, he wondered 'How can a wooden birdhouse survive the salt of the sea water? It should be in pieces, yet it's still intact!'

He noticed a small window carved into it. At that moment, an indescribable desire to look inside that window captured him. As he brought the birdhouse closer to his face, peering in, his eyes grew bigger and bigger from what he was seeing.

He saw himself on stage, singing his heart out to a multitude of people! Amazed by what he was beholding, he could not believe the happiness and contentment that filled him. Suddenly he wanted nothing more than to be on that stage. It was not enough to look at himself living his dream, he wanted to be there physically. The birdhouse sensed his desire and instantly pulled him deeper and deeper into itself through the window. Half of his head was supernaturally pulled inside! The desire to enter became stronger and stronger, the more he looked at himself on stage.

Everything inside him told him to let go, to surrender to what was happening. Half of his body was completely inside now! James pulled himself quickly out in fear, realizing how deep he had gone. He could not go through with it. It was too good to be true, he thought to himself. He dropped the birdhouse in fear. Before he knew what was happening to him, he was swept up by an invisible force, pulling him out of the ocean. The force caused him to levitate in the air and carried him back to the ship. As soon as his feet touched the deck, he held on to the railings with all his might. Shell-shocked, he slowly turned around and walked back to his cabin. He was wet, trembling from the cold and fear, but that did not matter to him. All he could think about as he stripped out of his wet clothes and into the warm bed was what he had just experienced and the things he had seen inside that birdhouse.

Hours later, James watched the sun coming up from his bedroom. He was pacing around his cabin, unable to sleep. It was impossible to sleep after what had happened. He tried to convince himself that it was all a dream, but he could not dismiss the damp pants and vest on the chair next to the dressing table. He kept remembering the sound of his name being whispered. A hand on his back startled him. Somebody was calling him. Who was it this time? He wondered. Turning around he found Jessica standing there.

"Hey, you," she smiled, "I've been calling and calling your name. You didn't answer when I knocked so I came in."

"It's all right," James said as he moved away from her and sat at the edge of the bed. Jessica could sense something was wrong. James was jumpy, almost frightened. She slowly walked to the edge of the bed and sat down. Tenderly, she stroked his back whilst looking at his face.

"What were you thinking about, that you could not even hear me come in?"

How in the world was he supposed to tell her what happened, when he didn't believe it himself? He chose to lie.

"It's nothing," he said faking a smile.

"It does not look like nothing to me. Look at you! You look as pale as a ghost," Jessica said, still stroking his back.

"I am just tired OK."

Jessica persisted. "James please tell me." He pushed Jessica's hand away and stood from the bed.

"I said it's nothing, now please stop pestering me!" he yelled.
There was silence in the room. Jessica could not believe it; James had yelled at her! She hadn't known James for long, but they had built such a strong bond and friendship in such a short space of time, that the hurt she felt moved right through her. She pressed her lips as hard as she could to keep herself from crying and stood up.

"I was only trying to help, I didn't mean to make a nuisance of myself, James." She turned her back and walked towards the door.

James was aghast at the realisation that he had actually shouted at her.

"Jessica, wait!" He ran towards the door and just managed to catch her before she walked out. He grabbed her by the arm. She turned and looked at him and he saw the pain written all over her face. He hated himself for wounding her. That had not been his intention. He just didn't know what to say to her. Leading her back towards the edge of the bed, he sat her down and proceeded to sit beside her, looking into her eyes. "I am so sorry. I didn't mean to snap at you. Please forgive me." With remorse all over his face, he reached out and put his arms around her.

"I thought we were supposed to be there for one another but now I just don't know, "Jessica said her voice breaking as she lifted her arms up. James sighed and stared at the floor. He knew he had to be honest when it came to her.

"You're right," he said holding her hand. "Something *is* bothering me but I can't talk about it right now. Everything is muddled up in my head and it's too much to handle. I just need to absorb it before I can talk to anyone about it. I promise, you will be the first person I talk to when I am ready."

Jessica looked intently at him. His eyes were desperately asking for her understanding and forgiveness. She could see that he genuinely felt horribly for what he had done. Looking into those eyes she could not help but acquiesce.

"You promise?" she asked with deep concern as she tipped her head up at him. He nodded. "You're forgiven," she said with a smile.

"Thank you," he smiled back at her. "So, what are you doing here anyway?" he asked.

"When you didn't show up for breakfast I decided to come and fetch you," she said, adding, "I guess you are not going to have breakfast with us after all."

"No, I am not." James replied. "Tell them I am sick from dinner last night."

"Adam will love that," Jessica chuckled. "Speaking of Adam, he wants us to go deep sea diving after breakfast, will you join us?"

"I am not going near that water ever again," James shot back at her and quickly stood up.

"What's that supposed to mean?" Jessica asked surprised.

"I am afraid of the water," he lied.
Jessica was starting to get annoyed at him.

"Why are you lying to me?" she asked as she stood up.

Ashamed of being caught in a lie he cast his eyes downwards, unable to face her. "Pretend I am not," he said.

"James I.....," Jessica started, but James interrupted her before she could finish her sentence.

"I really need to be alone, please." His eyes implored her not to ask any more questions but just let him be. Jessica understood without any more words being spoken.

"I'll leave you alone." Her irritation had died down. "See you when we get back. I am here for you when you're ready to talk," she said, turning her back and walking out of the door. James found himself alone again with his thoughts.

Jessica found Adam and Sarah finishing their breakfast in the dining room. She sat next to them. "James is not coming," she said as she dished for herself, a bowl of muesli.

"Why?" Sarah asked.

"He's sick. I think it's the ostrich he had," replied Jessica, praying that the two of them didn't realize she was lying through her teeth.

"Ha-ha," Adam laughed. "To think yesterday he was making fun of what I was eating."
"Be careful babe you might be next," Sarah said, looking at Adam and smiling at him. She was teasing him. Since they had been on this cruise, things between them were getting better and better, even when they were alone. The tension was gone. Talking was becoming easy and natural. She was starting to recognize her husband again.

"Oh no honey, my stomach is tough as teak," Adam said showing off his six-pack. Jessica and Sarah giggled, and he joined them. "So, girls are you ready for deep sea diving?" he asked in his best military imitation.

"Yes sir," the girls saluted.

After changing into the appropriate diving suit, Anton helped them put their gear on and gave them instructions on how to breathe under water. Nothing could have prepared them for what they were about to experience! It was truly more than they expected, or could imagine, beyond anything their eyes had ever seen. The sea was a different world filled with
beauty, silence and serenity. The extensive marine life included sea turtles, manta rays and a school of beautiful fish that painted the sea with all sorts of colours. Here they were, seeing all kinds of sea creatures, as if they had opened up a magical treasure box. Jessica took a picture of a seahorse using an underwater digital camera and managed to snap one of Sarah stroking a dolphin as it swam past her. Adam took a picture of an octopus of course. The sea show-cased the vast wonder of God's imagination through the creatures He had created. All three of them could not help but be enamoured by it all.

The three of them captured the moment with a plethora of pictures. First it was Jessica, who was taking pictures of Adam and Sarah waving, then Anton took pictures of the girls. Last but not least, Sarah took a picture of Adam and Jessica. She managed to squeeze herself in between them and take a picture of the three of them. Anton knew his way under water. If he hadn't been guiding them, the experience would never have been so memorable. He knew every nook and cranny that covered the most beautiful sea plants and flowers. The rocks shone like pearls. She had never seen anything like this in all her life. Her surroundings testified that only something heavenly and powerful could create such magnificence. She could not deny the presence of God all around her. She knew that her newfound friends were as moved by this experience as she was. In that moment Jessica wished James was with them. She hated the fact that he was missing out on such exquisite beauty. None of them wanted to go back to the surface, when Anton motioned with his finger that it was time to go up. Be-grudgingly, they surfaced and went back up to the yacht.

They were surprised to find James standing on the deck with towels. He had a big smile and Jessica was happy to see that his mood had changed. "So how was it?" he asked. Adam was the first to speak.

"It was incredible dude! You surely missed out! What a bummer about your tummy." Adam had turned into a kid, screaming, and hollering as he took the towel from James' hands. "Ask the girls they will tell you."

"Oh James, it was be-witching. Adam is right," Sarah said with exuberance. "The fish, the plants, I could have stayed there forever." she gushed.

"You would have to turn into a fish for that to happen," Jessica teased. "James, I wished you had come with us." Jessica said.

'Oh no thank you, I've had enough of that water for a lifetime,' he thought to himself.

"When I think about it, it brings me to tears," Jessica said as her eyes clouded.

"I know," Sarah said as she wiped tears from her own eyes. The men grinned patronisingly, and Adam rolled his eyes as the two ladies embraced whilst they let the tears fall without any shame.

"Well on that note I am going to change," Adam said with a big grin on his face. The open show of emotion was amusing for the guys. "Wait for me," Sarah said as she broke the embrace. "I completely forgot I am still in a wet suit."

"I need to go and change as well," Jessica said.

Sarah moved to Adam's side and they both walked to their rooms. Jessica was about to follow them when James held her back. "Can we talk?" he asked.

"Alright," she replied, looking at James. "Ready to tell me what's bothering you?"
"No, not just yet," he replied. "I need more time to process it. But I have decided to do nothing about it. I don't understand it and I can't explain it. So, I am not going to think about it," James said.

"Pretend that it never happened?" Jessica remarked.

"That's' the plan."

She could see he was lying to himself. "Do you think you can?"

"You are so intuitive."

Chapter 3

"It's a gift," she teased. "You didn't answer my question."

"I am going to try," James replied. "Starting with me going on a hike on the island with Anton tomorrow. While you guys were diving, I spoke to the stewardess at the bar, who told me about the hike. She said the island was uh…. what did you and Sarah say, oh yes *bewitching*," James said, mocking her. He turned his fingers into inverted commas.

"Ha-ha! Very funny," Jessica played along with a smile.

"Care to join me?"

Jessica declined, "No thanks. I don't want to do anything tiring after that diving."

"See you at dinner then."

"Actually James, I am going to have my dinner in my room. And I will tell Adam and Sarah from my cabin that I can't join them tonight. I am sure they are as exhausted as I am. How about you and I have dinner in my room?" Jessica asked.

"Cool," James replied.
"Great I will see you in an hour. Now I really need to get out of these wet clothes," she asserted, shaking, and running to her room. James nodded, smiling as he watched her scurry away. For the first time he wondered what it would have been like to have her as his real sister.

Sarah's Encounter

Sarah lay in bed wrapped in a towel, listening to her husband showering. 'I wonder what he would do if I slipped into the shower with him,' She thought to herself.' He would probably have a heart attack right there, or probably gallop out of the cubicle and cover his naked body,' she said as she laughed. Her mirth was laced with pain at the thought of her husband running away from her. 'But what if he didn't?' Sarah wondered. 'Things have been better ever since we came to the island. What if Adam took me in his arms kissed me and maybe...?' Sarah was brought back to reality by the phone ringing. She quickly grabbed it.

"Hello," she answered startled.

It was Jessica on the line. "Hey Sarah, are you OK?" Jessica asked.

"Yes, I am fine. Why do you ask?"

"You sound strange,"

"I was sleeping, the phone frightened me," Sarah lied.

"Oh..." Jessica replied.

"I am perfectly fine, nothing to worry about," Sarah lied some more. Her face turned pink, embarrassed at what she had just been thinking about her husband.

"Sorry didn't mean to scare you," Jessica replied with a giggle.

Chapter 3

"Listen, James and I are going to skip dinner in the dining room tonight, we are having it in my cabin. I am really tired from the diving. I hope you guys understand',' Jessica said apologetically.

"It's OK. I feel the same way. It's been a long day and I am terribly exhausted. Dinner in our rooms is a perfect idea. I will tell Adam. I am sure he will understand. He is probably exhausted as well. Thanks for thinking about it."

"You're welcome I guess," Jessica said, with a chuckle. "Goodnight Sarah, see you guys tomorrow,"

"Night dear, give my love to James."

"Will do" Jessica said and dropped the phone.

Adam came out of the shower with a towel around his waist. "Who was that?"

"Jessica, she is tired from the diving. So, she and James are having dinner in her cabin." His wife explained.

"Oh," he said with a huge grin on his face.

"It's not what you are thinking," Sarah amused.

"What?" Adam said, throwing his hands in the air. He was smiling from ear to ear. It was clear what he was thinking. "I didn't say anything."

"No, but you are thinking it," she shook her forefinger at Adam.

"Oh, come on Sarah, they are having dinner *alone. In her room,*" Adam answered. The grin never left his face.

"They are just friends, Adam," Sarah grabbed a pillow and threw it at him. Adam ducked out of the way.

"You missed," he mocked, picking the pillow from the floor, and throwing it back at Sarah playfully.

"Ow!" she screamed as it hit her. She took the pillow and held it close to her chest. "Jessica sees James as a brother."

"And how do you know? Did she say anything to you?" he interrogated her.

"No but a woman knows these things, we know when you are interested in us, just like I knew you were interested in me," she said with playful self-satisfaction.

He refuted her claim boldly, "You did not!"

"Oh yes, I did" Sarah replied coyly.

"Well Miss Sarah, I knew that you had a big crush on yours truly," he teased.

"You couldn't have," Sarah said her eyes as wide as a deer in headlights.

"But I did," Adam said mischievously. "You smiled, and your face turned a cherry pink when I entered the room. A giggle would slip out of your mouth each time I gave you a comment." He was enjoying the teasing.

"You remember?" she asked. Her face had turned pink.

"I remember everything."
The room went silent as husband and wife looked at each other with love. Sarah wanted more than anything to hold Adam at that moment. She slowly moved from the bed and walked towards her husband. He baulked and took a step back. The time had long passed when Adam questioned himself as to what made him abhor his wife's touch. It made no sense at all, except perhaps, when he considered his own guilty conscience. Was there an honest part of his psyche that reviled his philandering and made him feel too unclean to be with her? Could it be he was projecting his own revulsion with himself onto Sarah? He wished he knew.

"You better go and take that shower," he said uncomfortably.

"Of course," she answered in embarrassed sadness. "I am sorry Adam, it's my fault, I don't know what I was thinking." Adam didn't say a word. He turned his back on her and started getting dressed. She quickly went to the shower. Tears flooded her eyes. 'Will I ever learn?' she scolded herself. The water was running, and Adam couldn't hear his wife crying.

After a while he called out to her from the room.

"Jessica came up with a good idea; I am beat. Should I order something for the both of us?"

"Yes, thank you," she called out, trying to speak as calmly as she could, wiping the tears from her eyes. Adam had no idea what was happening in the shower and that was how Sarah wanted it. She enjoyed the soothing effect of the water cascading all over her body. 'I can't believe that I tried to reach out to him! What was I going to do when I reached him?' she asked herself? "Kiss him? As if that could ever happen!" she muttered angrily. "This island is playing with my mind." She stayed longer than she should have in the shower, not wanting any trace of her crying to be seen. By the time she slipped into her gown and came back to the room, her husband was asleep. She sighed in relief. At least she didn't have to face him just now though she was sure of one thing; she would have to face the tension when he woke up. 'Looks like the diving really wiped him out,' she thought to herself. There was a knock at the door.

"Room service," the crew member called from outside. Sarah opened for him, and he brought the tray in.

"Thank you."

"You're welcome, Ma'am," he said as he left.

She tried to wake her husband up, but it was no use. He was out like a candle. She had her dinner, then lay next to him, falling into a long, deep sleep. When she woke up, she realized Adam's plate was empty. She smiled and looked at her husband lying next to her. He must have woken up. Slowly she reached out and grabbed her wristwatch from the side table. It was eleven o'clock at night. She was surprised at being up. She would usually be asleep around this time, but for some reason she was wide awake and very restless tonight. Something was telling her to go up to the upper deck. She tried to ignore this gnawing feeling that would not leave her alone and to force herself to sleep. Around twelve she finally gave up and walked briskly up to the deck. What was she doing here in the middle of the night? What was so important that she had to see it, she wondered. Something told her she desperately needed to be there.

"Sarah," a voice was calling out to her. 'Or was it a whisper? she wasn't sure.

"Hello, who is there?"

"Sarah," she heard the hushed tone again. "Sarah." She realized the whisper was coming from the sea. Unable to stop herself, she looked down over the railing. Had someone fallen overboard? She quickly looked down from the deck, frightened for the person that might have fallen, but realized there was no one in the water. What the hell is going on here, she wondered. She began to feel very afraid. She was about to run back to her room, but she felt a strong force keeping her from moving.

"Sarah," she heard someone or something calling her again. The soft spoken voice came again from the water. She leaned even further than before. The whisper was hypnotizing and so powerful. "Sarah." There it was again, she discerned. She was afraid but captivated and mesmerized all at the same time. Whatever was happening or going to happen to her, she had no control over it. Something bigger and more powerful than anything she had ever experienced had taken her over. She felt a strong pull to bend further down and look at the night sea. It was still, but she sensed it was alive. Something in the water was calling her. "Whatever you want me to do, I will do it, she whispered in the air. In an instance she was pulled over the deck and deep down into the sea. The force pulled her with such speed that it left her powerless. Deeper and deeper, she was pulled until she hit the sandy bottom.

Suddenly whatever was pulling her had left. She was at the bottom of the ocean. Why am I alive and why can I walk under water? I must have drowned. Could this be heaven? Sarah wondered. Fear gripped her. Have I really died? she asked herself. That could be the only explanation she concluded. Suddenly a sense of tranquillity swept all around her. The fear went away. She didn't know what was happening, but she knew everything was going to be alright. Sarah noticed a birdhouse lying on the ground as she looked around at her surroundings. She slowly picked it up. What was a birdhouse doing under water? Why was she so drawn to it? She turned the little house, examining every detail. She was subconsciously looking for something and then suddenly she found it. The birdhouse had a window which she was immediately drawn to look inside. As she looked, her eyes grew bigger, and she gasped in astonishment from what she was seeing.

She saw Adam. He had his arms around her, and he was kissing her in their house. No this could not possibly be happening! She thought to herself, I must have died and now I am reliving my memories. But this does not feel like a memory, she realized. The more she watched herself with her husband, the deeper the ache and want for Adam increased. More than anything in her life, she wanted to be in that birdhouse kissing him.

Sarah felt compelled to press deeper into the window. The house was calling her, making her dreams come true. She knew the house was offering her what she had always wanted more than anything in the whole world. She was being offered it on a silver platter, all she had to do was take it. Sarah surrendered to her want and pushed herself deeper into the house. She felt the house pulling her into the window until half her body was completely in. She didn't realize what was happening to her. Whatever was happening had complete and utter control over her. She needed and wanted to be with her husband again.

Suddenly her senses came back to her. It was as if the house was giving her a choice. Allowing her to decide whether to carry on moving or go back. She made her choice out of fright. This was too good to be true, there must be a
catch, she deliberated. She quickly drew her head back from the window and dropped the house on the sand. Sarah had rejected the offer that was given to her.

The powerful force pulled her up to the surface, and back to the deck. Her gown was dripping wet. She was shaking. Uncontrollable tears of relief started falling down her cheeks. She was happy to be alive and totally afraid and amazed from her encounter. What did this all mean? Sarah wondered, while walking back to her room. As soon as she entered the cabin, she quickly changed her gown and slipped into the covers next to her husband. The rest of the night she watched Adam sleeping. She couldn't stop crying. She muffled her tears with a pillow. Everything that had happened to her was too overwhelming. It had left her drained and confused. She thought, how am I ever going to begin to explain this to Adam? Will he even believe me? Her entire body was shaking, not from the cold but from utter shock and disbelief.

Adam woke up and found Sarah sitting on the sofa staring at him. He realized she had been crying. "Are you OK?" he asked. He was worried.

"We need to talk," she said, her hands shaking. He had his suspicions about why his wife wanted to talk to him. Lifting himself from the bed, he pushed himself back until he leaned on the headboard.

"Sarah if this is about yesterday, let's just forget it, I forgive you, OK?" He could not hide his irritation. He didn't understand why it was necessary to rehash everything that happened yesterday.
"You forgive me?" Sarah said dumbfounded.

"Yes, I understand how you get carried away sometimes. I mean we are on holiday and these things happen. You know I get carried away sometimes too. So, you are forgiven," Adam said in a patronizing tone.

Sarah looked at Adam and yelled out, "Adam you need to get yourself another room or I will move in with Jessica!" She was boiling in anger. The nerve of this man! Forgiving me because I wanted to touch him! If I had remained in that birdhouse, I would be with the Adam that loved me and not this insensitive boy! Rage that had been pent up for years was bubbling like a burning volcano inside of her.

"What? I don't understand?" Adam replied in shock.

"I am serious," Sarah answered sternly and trying by all means to calm down.

"Sarah, you can't be serious." Adam replied mockingly. "You and I have been doing great. You made a mistake. I have forgiven you. So can we please just drop it?" he yelled out furiously.

"My husband forgives me for wanting to kiss him!" Sarah yelled from the top of her lungs. "Where have you heard of such a thing!?" she continued. Adam was surprised by Sarah's response.
"I thought you understood," he replied. He was confused by Sarah's angry outburst. "I mean you have always been such a trooper."

If Adam called her a trooper one more time, she was going to have a fit, she thought to herself. "You need to talk to Anton to get you your own cabin or I will do it myself!" Sarah shouted back at him.

"Sarah what will Jessica and James think?" Adam replied, trying as hard as he could to calm himself down. Screaming at his wife was not getting him anywhere he realized. "Please be reasonable," he pleaded, while standing up from the bed.

Embarrassed at her outburst Sarah lowered her voice and said, "I've had to face people gossiping about your infidelities for as long as I can remember. It's your turn to face the music," she said in a serious tone.

"Sarah please, you are being ridiculous!" Adam replied in frustration.

"I am being ridiculous?" she laughed sarcastically. "What if I try to kiss you again? Will that be ridiculous?" she asked.

"What! You want to kiss me?" he asked uncomfortably.

"You are my husband, aren't you?" she replied condescendingly.

"What has gotten in you? Adam asked in a reprimanding tone. "You know how I feel," Adam continued but Sarah did not allow him to finish his sentence.

"Oh yes Adam, I know how you feel! You have made that quite clear to me!" she said sharply.

"I don't understand what is going on here, but I don't like it," he replied in anger.
"I don't know Adam, maybe I have finally lost my mind," she replied in a hostile tone.

"You're right, maybe we need separate rooms," he replied sternly. "Get yourself together Sarah or I will..." Adam was unable to finish his sentence.

Sarah stormed towards the door while he was speaking, grabbed the door, opened it and said insultingly, "You will what? Cheat on me?" then she stormed out of the cabin without even looking back.

She walked back to the deck in frustration and was startled by James starring at the water. She prayed that James did not see the anger all over her face. He seemed not to notice, thank God. Something was on his mind, she realised. "James, how are you feeling today?" she tried to conjure up a smile.

"How am I feeling?" James asked in confusion. Suddenly it dawned on him that he had lied to them. "Oh, the stomach bug. I am fine," he replied, trying not to look Sarah in the eye. "It was just a one-day thing. Jessica and I last night wanted something different from the delicacies we have been eating, so we went for something totally different. We were eating all the junk food you can possibly imagine. Pizza, waffles, ice cream and chocolate! I mean you name it; we ate it, and I did not get sick. We had a ball acting like kids," he replied with a smile.

Sarah noticed the bag on the floor. "You are leaving?" Sarah asked.

"On a camping trip," he replied. "Anton and I are going to explore the island. I need some time out to think about some things," he continued. "Anton was telling me how peaceful it is. It's the perfect place to do some thinking."

"I can use some peace and quiet too," Sarah answered sadly. Suddenly a thought came to her mind. "Maybe I can come with you?"

"What...why?" James asked. "I mean forgive me, but you don't seem like the outdoors type," he continued.

"I am not, Adam and I had a fight," she said with a sad sigh. "I just need to be away from him for a while."

"I don't know Sarah, I am not going to be good company, if you know what I mean," James replied.

"I understand." And she did, more than they both realized. They had both had the same experience, and the two of them had no idea. "Please James, I really need this."

James could see the desperation in her sad eyes and could hear it in her voice. He could not help but feel for her. "OK," he replied with a smile. "Go pack a bag, I will ask Anton to wait for you."

Sarah hugged him. "Thank you, James," she said, with a genuine smile. She ran to her room and started packing a few of her clothes in a duffel bag, without looking at Adam.
"What are you doing?" Adam asked.

"You don't have to move anymore. Anton and James are exploring the island and I am going with them." She was not asking but telling him.

"Just like that?" Adam asked in confused anger.

She walked to the door and opened it. "Yes Adam, just like that," Sarah replied cuttingly and walked out, slamming the door behind her.

Adam watched James and Sarah hugging and saying goodbye to Jessica. He saw them climb out of the cruise ship, stepping carefully into the speed boat. He was watching from a distance. Adam started walking towards Jessica, when he was sure Sarah and James were on their way to the shore. "Well, I guess it's just you and me," Adam said, while standing next to Jessica.

"Yeah, I guess," Jessica replied. "I am sorry you missed them leave," she said. "I am surprised you didn't join James and Sarah on the hike. She looked upset when she left," Jessica reflected.

"I was not invited. Things are tense between us," Adam replied. "I didn't want to crowd her space."

Jessica responded with a nod, showing her understanding. "What about you? Why didn't you go?" Adam asked Jessica.

"I am too wiped out from the diving,"

"So, what are we going to do with ourselves for two whole days?" Adam asked flirtatiously

"Adam you better behave yourself. I am not that kind of a` women. Things can get really ugly between us. I will slap the white off your skin and turn you black in a second if you carry on like this and besides Sarah and I have become friends on this trip. I have no problem at all in telling her what her husband was getting up to while she was away". Jessica said mercilessly.

"I am really sorry Jessica. I went too far. I had a really bad argument with Sarah and I was not thinking. Can you please keep this between us? I would really like it if we could start again as friends. I feel so ashamed.

He tried to make light of the situation and make her smile. "I did not mean to step on the lioness tale."

It worked. She smiled and growled like a lioness. Aarghghgh Don't do it again."

Chapter 3

"I won't, not ever again" He promised.

" Anyway, I intend to pamper myself at the beauty parlour,"

"I am going to the games room to try out every game in there. Care
to join me and pamper yourself tomorrow?"
"Sure, sounds like fun," Jessica replied with a smile.

The day went by very quickly. Jessica and Adam played every game
they could lay their hands on. First, they played a game of pool,
from there they moved to the bumper cars. Jessica enjoyed the
bumper cars more than any other game. They were like two kids in
a candy room. "I don't remember being so happy in my life," she
yelled from the top of her lungs as she chased after Adam.
"Yeah, it's great to just let go," he called out as he quickly reversed
his car and bumped straight into the car she was driving. Jessica
laughed from the top of her lungs as he smashed into her again.

"Forgetting everything and just being," she screamed out of
delight. She chased after Adam and hit the rear of his car.

"For a woman you are alright," Adam shouted to Jessica.

"Thanks Adam. I take that as a compliment. Most of my friends think
I am boring," she hollered back and rammed into his car again.

Around two in the afternoon they had lunch at the upper deck. The
rest of the day was spent tanning and swimming, drinking cocktails

and listening to the reggae music which was playing in the background.

Adam's Encounter

Adam was having a restless night. He could not sleep. He had dinner with Jessica in the dining room and went back to his cabin. He thought sleep would come easily after the swimming he had done and could not understand why it didn't. I must still be angry with Sarah, he thought to himself. A walk around the ship might tire me out.

Adam walked to the upper deck without even realizing it. For some reason, this particular night he was drawn to the ocean. Looking at the deep dark sea while holding on to the rails, he felt mesmerized by the water. Suddenly out of nowhere he heard someone calling his name from the sea.

"Adam."

It was a spell binding whisper that removed all his defences the minute he heard it. Enchanted by the whisper, Adam bent further down, his eyes fixed into the night ocean. No one had ever called his name like that. It was entrancing, as if the owner of the voice knew him. He felt accepted for who he was and loved unconditionally. He had never experienced such allegiance and appreciation in his life, not even from Sarah. There was no judgment at all from the voice. He felt wanted in the purest form. Adam wanted more than anything to be with the voice.

His heart was at ease knowing he could depend on whoever it was calling out to him, the voice had the solutions to all issues of life. The voice only wanted to help him and would never fail or abandon him.
"Where are you?" He called out into the night. "Please don't leave me."

 He was gripped by the murmur. He had no desire or ability to resist. He no longer belonged to himself but to the voice. For the first time in his life, he truly felt free. In an instance, he felt an explosion of power pulling him over the deck and straight into the water, gripping and pulling him with dynamic force and leaving him at the bottom of the ocean. Adam willingly accepted what was happening to him, reason had flown out of the window. He didn't even wonder why he could breathe and walk under water! None of those thoughts came to his mind. All that mattered was the whisper he heard. He had to find the owner of the voice. That was the only thing that mattered to him.

Adam walked around the bottom of the ocean looking for the owner of the voice but found instead, a birdhouse made of wood. Drawn to the wooden house, he felt the need to pick it up. As soon as he had the little house in his hands, an overflowing excitement came over him. He felt as if the birdhouse had all the answers he was looking for. He noticed a tiny window and was immediately drawn to look inside it. The house was talking to him, asking him to look and see the deep secrets it was carrying. Without any resistance but with a deep desire and interest he had never experienced before, Adam looked inside the window.

He saw himself and Sarah in a passionate embrace. He could not believe his eyes. She was kissing him, and he was responding. It's me, and I am actually responding and enjoying her touch, Adam thought to himself in amazement. Only in another world could I not be repulsed by my wife's touch, he discerned with deep longing. Only in a dream, he thought with regret. Suddenly all Adam cared about was being with Sarah. More than anything in the world, I want to be in this perfect world, Adam thought, as his desire grew more and more. Everything he kept hidden from everybody took over. This new reality is unfolding right in front of me, he reasoned. A world, where I am the perfect husband. A world where Sarah is happy, he thought to himself. His desire to be different overtook him. His desire to be free from his weaknesses moved him closer and closer to the window. A world where I am not afraid to love and be loved. A world where everything I touch does not turn into crap. The tip of his head entered the window. He did not realize what was happening to him. In a world where I win for a change, he concluded, while half of his head disappeared into the house. If only I could find a way to be there, Adam contemplated, as half of his upper body disappeared into the house.

Only his waist and legs were still visible in the ocean. Adam suddenly realized what was happening to him. Nothing good ever happens in my life, he thought. Why should it start now? This was a trap, he concluded in his mind and quickly out of trepidation, he pulled himself out of the birdhouse window. Immediately he was ripped from the bottom of the ocean and was brought up to the surface by the same energy that had drew him into the ocean. Before he knew what was happening, he found himself floating in the air and being carried by an invisible mighty force, back to the deck of the ship. He started running without looking back and did not stop until he was safely back in his room. In disbelief, he asked the only question he could ask himself in his mind. What the hell happened to me? Knowing fully well no one will ever have the answer to that question.

Jessica's Encounter

It was a beautiful glorious morning when Jessica woke up from her sleep. She smiled as she watched the sun from her window. It's a beautiful day to pamper myself, she thought. Every day she woke up with a smile on her face and slept like a baby every night, the tonic-being the ocean waves lulling her to sleep every night. This cruise had been exactly what she needed. She had done some snorkelling. Yesterday she had played games with Adam and today she was going to spoil herself by going to the beauty parlour. "Can a holiday get any better!" she thought out loud. She could not help but hum from being so happy, while having her morning coffee.

The phone began ringing. She placed the coffee cup on the side table and answered the phone. "Hello," she said with a smile.

"Hi Jessica," Adam said nervously.

"Hey Adam, how are you doing this morning?" Jessica replied with sensitivity. She recognized the nervousness in Adam's voice.

"Not so good. I am not going to have breakfast and dinner with you today,"

"Why?"

He hesitated before telling the lie. "Stomach bug."

"You too?!" she said in total disbelief. "First it was James, now you! How strange that the bug affects you days after you had the octopus. I guess it will be me next." She knew he was lying.

"There is no reason to be sarcastic," Adam responded. His face had turned red on the other end of the phone.

"There is no reason to lie either," she replied. Adam could not say another word. "Maybe you should have thought of a better lie," she said sympathetically.

"Maybe I should have." Adam responded with a sigh.

"Adam what's wrong?" She was worried.

"I am not sick. I am still upset about the fight with Sarah, and I just need time to be alone," he lied again. This time it was a better lie and Jessica believed him.

"I am sorry Adam," she said trying to make him feel better. "Do you want to talk?"

"No," he responded quickly.

"You want Sarah."

"Yes, more than you know," he answered in a whisper.
"I understand," Jessica responded out of sympathy for her friend. "They will be back tomorrow. You guys can talk then,"

"Yeah, I guess."

Adam was never a man lost for words. Jessica was surprised by his response. She could not help but feel for the guy.
"Listen you guys have each other. You don't know how lucky you are. Many people would kill just to have someone to love. It's a gift, cherish it, and fight for it," She said.

Tears welled up in Adams eyes as the picture of him kissing his wife with such want and pleasure came to his mind. If only Jessica knew what she was doing to him, he thought.

"Ah thanks for the advice but I have to go," he said trying to hold back his tears.

"Will I see you for dinner?" Jessica asked.

Thank God she doesn't realize that I am almost in tears, he thought to himself. "I don't think so," he responded quickly.

"That bad huh?" she asked in sympathy.

"Yep, see you Jess," he answered. Adam dropped the phone and walked to the fitness centre. He tried every piece of equipment in the room, exercising and sweating until he had no strength to think about the events of last night.

"There is no reason for me to have breakfast in the dining room if I am going to eat alone, Jessica thought to herself while holding the phone and listening to the dialling tone in her ear. Whatever is upsetting Adam must be really bad and I wish I could help, but I have to respect his privacy", Jessica said thinking out loud. She called room service. She heard the voice of a woman with an island, velvet accent on the other end.

"Room service. How can I be of assistance?"

"Hello. Can I have breakfast in my cabin this morning?"

"What would you like miss?" The hostess asked.

"For starters I will have a fruit salad with muesli and vanilla yogurt. Then I will have toasted brown bread, an omelette with onions, mushrooms and chicken livers, with pineapple juice please,"

"I will personally bring it to your room miss," the hostess responded graciously.

Chapter 3

"Thank you. What is your name?"

"It's Grace Miss,"

"That's a beautiful name,"

"Thank you, Miss. Will you have dessert as well?" Grace asked.
"Well, I am on holiday," Jessica said with a smile "I will have a waffle with ice cream and some syrup." She was laughing to herself, enjoying every bit of her holiday.

"May I suggest some strawberries on top of the ice cream?"

"Thanks Grace. You are so sweet," Jessica responded with a smile on her face. "I would love that, God bless."

"Thank you miss and same to you," Grace replied in appreciation to her kindness.

"Do you and Mr Adam have anything planned for today that I may be of assistance? I am Anton's assistant and have taken over his duties on the ship while he is away," Grace said.

"Well I was planning to pamper myself today by going to the beauty parlour. I will not be seeing Adam today."

"May I suggest something Miss? How about going to the steam room or Jacuzzi first, have a massage and end your day by having a manicure and pedicure?"

"Oh wow, that would be fantastic," Jessica said in delight.

"I will have everything ready for you when you come in Miss."

"Thanks, I really appreciate everything you do for me Grace," Jessica said with gratitude.
"You're most welcome Miss, and please don't hesitate to call if you need anything else."

Jessica screamed in excitement as she dropped the phone. This is going to be an awesome day, she thought to herself. Nothing in the world can ever make me want to leave this place. I am so glad I came. If only I could stay.

Home was such a distant reality. Being here felt like home to her. It was at her real home where she felt like a stranger, where she felt she didn't belong. Life was supposed to be like this every day. It should be lived in excitement and happiness. Will I be this happy when I am married to Derrick, she wondered then quickly pushed that thought away before it could steal her joy.

It had been an incredible day for her. She reflected on the events as she lay in her comfortable bed later that night. It had truly been a day of pampering. She had spoilt herself thoroughly at the beauty parlour and spa. Her whole body felt rejuvenated. After such a fantastic day, all she was waiting for was her beauty sleep. You would think after such a relaxing massage I would be asleep by now, she thought. Sleep was not coming as easily this evening. She was feeling the opposite of relaxation actually. She became more and more restless. By midnight she threw off her covers and took a walk. She walked to the deck of the ship and found herself looking at the night ocean that usually lulled her to sleep every night. She felt mesmerized by the sight of it. As she looked at the sea, she could actually sense its restlessness and the pervading aura of impending events that it exuded although didn't know what that was. The more she looked at the ocean the more deeply drawn she was to it. There was something different about this sea tonight. She could sense it. From out of nowhere she heard her name being whispered into the atmosphere.

"Jessica."

Her whole body tensed in excitement and fear. She turned her head, waiting to see if someone would come towards her, but nobody came. Maybe I am imagining things, she concluded. No one is calling my name. She was trying to convince herself. Suddenly she heard her name being called again.

"Jessica."

"Is there anybody there?" she called into the night. No one answered.

"Jessica." The whisper was now close to her right ear. It felt as if the night air was calling to her. The back of her neck prickled. In shock, she quickly turned around but found nobody there. She suddenly felt an aura accompanying the whisper. It was gentle yet very powerful. She could sense the presence's authority and sovereignty.

The entity and whisper overwhelmed her to the core of her soul. She started feeling a sensation of love, calmness and bliss moving in and all around her. She had never known these powerful feelings in all her life. She was overcome by something beyond her. She heard her name being called again.
"Jessica."
The voice took total control over. She knew she belonged to nobody else but this mysterious power. She sensed the celestial life force knew her better than she knew herself. It even knew what she didn't know about herself, her life and destiny. It could lead her to her crowning glory. She knew she was around something immaculate and splendid. This phenomenon took over her entire being. She had lost all her willpower. Her only option being around such superiority was to surrender. It felt as if God himself had paid a personal visit to her. Wait a minute, she wondered. Am I having a personal encounter with the Heavenly Father Himself?

Again, she heard her name being whispered. "Jessica.'

' Realizing that the whisper was coming from the ocean, she sensed that the presence and whisper were the same thing. She knew this was a friend that would never turn away from her, a friend that remembered her pain and the tears she had cried. A friend that fought her battles, which was still fighting for the dreams she had given up on. She recognized this atmosphere. It was the same spirit she felt each time she prayed. Excitement and eagerness to be led by the whisper took instant control over her. The spirit was divine. The spirit was God. She knew this deep inside within her soul. Out of devotion, adoration and complete submission, Jessica bent over more and more from the deck.

She closed her eyes and prayed. "Creator of heaven and earth. Creator of the sea. I am here, do as you wish."

As soon as the words left her lips, she felt the mighty presence engulfing her, carrying her by the speed of lightning off the deck of the ship and into the ocean. She was being carried with such intensity to the bottom of the ocean. Fear should have taken over at this moment, but Jessica felt nothing of the sort. Tranquillity she had never felt before, moved all around her body and soul as her feet landed at the bottom of the ocean. Logic had flown away. She sensed deep within her soul that this was meant to happen. Walking among the fish and breathing in water, Jessica felt her foot kick something hidden in the sand. She was drawn and fascinated by this object instantly.

Jessica found herself bending down and digging in the sand with her hands. She didn't understand why she was digging but something deep within her was telling her to dig until she found the object secreted away in the sand. It didn't take long for her to realise that the object which had taken all her attention and interest was a birdhouse. Jessica started to examine the wooden house attentively. What was a wooden birdhouse doing in the ocean? Why had it not decayed from the saltiness of the sea? In her exploration of the house Jessica noticed a window on it. Her eyes were drawn to look inside. They grew wider and wider in utter amazement at what she was seeing inside the birdhouse at that instant!

She saw what her eyes had longed to see, what she had envied with every breath she took on this earth. She saw herself in the arms of a man she loved and who loved her in return. They were in bed together chatting with their clothes on. There was a bible between them. It looked like they were having a conversation about a revelation they had received from the bible. Jessica noticed that in the vision, she was wearing a wedding ring. She was finally in the arms of the man who would love her for the rest of her life. The man she had prayed to God for. Could this be really happening to her?

She was seeing what she had imagined and dreamed of all her life. Yet it never looked as beautiful as it looked in this vision. The man, who would open a world she longed to be part of, had finally arrived in her life. A world where her body that had become a desert thirsty for affection, would now feel the oasis of a man's kisses and touch. A world where her womb would carry life and a baby would slip through her thighs. A world where she would feel the mouth of a baby tugging on her nipple as she breastfed. A world where she would finally experience what every woman her age around the world enjoyed. The experience of being with a man in the most intimate way. To fit with a man, the way clothing fitted on a body. To be beheld by a man's eyes as her mirror beheld her every morning and night when she discarded her clothing. For her scent to be in a man's memory as the fragrance of a rose stayed in a woman's mind. To bloom as a flower when experiencing the kiss of the sun's rays for the very first time. She saw herself in bed with a man she knew was her husband. She watched the vision of her dreams coming to life in front of her very eyes.

A deep longing encompassed her. To watch this and not be part of it was too much to bear. She had been a spectator too many times in her life. Seeing other people, friends living their lives and dreams. Watching younger women married discarding the cocoon of innocence. Seeing life after life coming into the world through other women's wombs except by her. She had been a bystander for far too long. Now, more than life itself, she wanted to be a participant! Jessica started to feel every cell in her body ache like a burning furnace to be part of what she was seeing with her eyes! Feeling the burning desire inside her, the house started to push her closer and closer to the window. Her face went through the window. All her inhibitions had disappeared. A deep desire fuelled by lonely nights and empty days had taken over. A deep stillness filled her senses, allowing her to accept the magic that was happening to her. She felt the house starting to propel her even further inside itself with such want, wanting to give her all she ever desired. The house dragged her in without any reluctance from her until half of her body was inside.

The realization of what was happening brought her back to her senses. She could see both of her arms inside the house. In fear she started to pull herself out. As soon as her head came out, the omnipotent force started to scoop her up and carry her up to the surface. The invisible life form gently carried her in the air. She could not believe what was happening. She was levitating in the air! Her emotions moved between fear and excitement as she came closer and closer to the ship. The intangible essence placed her back on deck. Jessica did not remember walking back to her room or taking her wet night gown off. She could not remember climbing into her bed. Her brain activity had been temporarily frozen. She did everything without any memory. She was hypnotized. She was in utter shock of what she had experienced. Jessica didn't blink once throughout the night.

Chapter 3

Chapter **4**

Sarah and James Return

*T*he sun appeared in the sky, greeting the world and bringing a new day as a gift. James and Sarah were coming from their excursion. Jessica and Adam watched them come on deck. Everybody looked preoccupied and you could cut the tension with a knife.

"Hey guys," James said, giving a hug to both of them. He could see in both Jessica and Adam's eyes that something was wrong.

" So how was the island?" Jessica asked Sarah, who had been quiet since she came on deck.

"It was fine," she smiled. "Gave me time to think," she looked at Adam with eyes that held deep painful secrets.

"Just fine?" Jessica asked, out of surprise. "I mean you are a nature lover like I am and all you can say is fine!" Jessica gave Sarah a suspicious look.

"Jessica is right. You have been acting strange lately. What is really going on with you?" Adam asked.

"Oh, I am sorry I guess I am just tired, but it was beautiful." Sarah realized her simple answer might cause the others to think something was upsetting her, which was true. She had to rescue the situation before they started asking her questions. "The scenery was breath-taking, you should have come," she said, looking at Jessica and completely ignoring her husband.

Jessica started having a flash back from last night. "Maybe you are right,"

James noticed the colour leave her face. "Why?" James asked. "Didn't you and Adam have a good time?" he asked, concern written all over his face.

"We had a great time," Jessica replied.
"We sure did," Adam said, remembering the games they played. Then he started to remember his encounter in the water and the smile left his face. He went silent. Sarah was the first to notice.

"Are you OK?" she asked.

Chapter 4

Adam realized his silence could make his wife, start to ask questions. He had to think fast.

"Yesterday I was not feeling well, bad stomach bug. Just thinking about my *ordeal*," he said, using his fingers as inverted commas.

"Actually guys, I just wanted to say hi," Jessica said, looking for an escape route. She lied; "I am not feeling well. I think I may have caught the bug myself. So, I will be in my room most of the time."

"I see," James said suspiciously. He looked straight into Jessica's eyes, to see if she was lying. Jessica looked flustered the moment their eyes met. She could not lie to James. Guilt was written all over her face.

"You both had the stomach bug?" James remarked. It was a rhetorical question. "What a coincidence," he said, looking at Adam. Hoping to sense if he was lying or telling the truth. He looks as if he is hiding something too. Could what happened to me, have happened to them? James wondered.

"Something is up with you two and it has nothing to do with a stomach bug," James said.

As soon as the words left James' mouth Sarah's eyes were fixed on her husband, pain written all over her face. It dawned to Adam what she was thinking. Jumping to conclusions. Sarah yelled in anger mixed with sadness, "How could you Adam?"

"It's not what you think," Adam said. He moved towards Sarah.

"Oh yes, it is," she shouted.

"Not this time," Adam said as he reached his wife and held on to her shoulders.

"Let go of me!" she shrieked as she pushed his hands away.

"You slept with her!" Sarah roared at her husband. Tears were flowing from Sarah's eyes.

"What! You think Adam and I slept together?" Jessica asked, bewildered by what she was hearing.

"Don't patronize me, Jessica. I know my husband," Sarah said bluntly.
"But you don't know me," Jessica replied firmly. "I would *never* do that! How *dare* you accuse me of such a thing!" Jessica shouted back with indignation written all over her face.

"Jessica, no woman can resist him. So, let's not pretend here OK!" Sarah said scornfully, wiping tears from her face.

"Now you listen here!" Jessica screamed back. "I am a decent woman. I would never do that ever! Now I see how little you think of me." She felt angry and hurt. She thought she had made a new friend in Sarah. "Believe whatever you want. Just to make things clear, we aren't friends anymore." She was furious with Sarah, enough to slap her. She stayed really still resisting the temptation.

Chapter 4

"Sarah, I swear on my life I did not sleep with this woman," Adam said. His face red with embarrassment.

"Alright guys, let's just calm down," James said as he walked towards Sarah. He stood between Sarah and Jessica.

"Sarah, something is up with these two, but they did not sleep together," he said sincerely.

"How do you know James? You were with me on the island remember!" Sarah yelled, fresh tears flowing down her face.

"Listen I *know* Jessica did not do this," James said, pleading with Sarah.

"He's right. You are embarrassing yourself and me. The entire crew on the ship can hear your howling," Adam said, seething with anger. Sarah was neither scared nor moved.

"Shut up Adam! I have had enough of you. You make me sick!" Her eyes fixed on her husband.

Sarah's focus went back to James, standing next to her. "They had the perfect opportunity to..."

Unable to take another second of watching his friend being accused of a lie, James blurted out, "She is a virgin!"

Sarah stopped right in her tracks and did not finish her sentence. "What?" she said almost in a whisper out of shock.

"She is saving herself for marriage," James continued.

"I didn't know," Sarah said apologetically. All the anger drained out of her by the news, while Jessica's anger had reached its boiling point!

"Well now you do!" she said glaring at Sarah. "You all do!" Jessica shouted at the top of her lungs.

"I am sorry, I had no choice," James pleaded.

"Save it," Jessica yelled at James. "I don't want to hear anything from you! I told you that in confidence and you thought you had a right to share it with everybody." James' face went red, and he kept silent.

"Yes, I am a virgin and it's none of anyone's business!" she exclaimed, as she looked at everybody. Humiliation was moving up her spine to the core of her soul, tears silently dripping down her face. Everyone kept silent.

"Yes, I am acting strange because something happened to me, on this damn island!" Jessica yelled. "Something I don't feel like sharing with any of you," she said emotionally. "But since you and James seem to think you can be judge and jury, let's talk about your actions." She turned to Sarah. "You left your husband on a yacht

117

and went exploring. Why didn't you take your husband with you, huh? You are on holiday together! Did any of us ask you why you did that?'' she asked mockingly. Sarah kept silent. ''I should just slap you,'' Jessica said, glaring at her. Sarah's' head drooped out of shame. "As for you Mr Detective,'' Jessica said to James. "We both know you never had a stomach bug, don't we James?'' she said accusingly.

"Yes,'' was the only word James could utter from his mouth. He was mortified.

''Let's face it!' We are all keeping secrets here!'' Jessica shrieked. ''Well now that I have been humiliated enough. I will be going.'' She stomped off to her room, crying uncontrollably.

"Well, that went well!'' Adam said sarcastically. ''I hope you are proud of yourself Sarah."

''I am sorry I thought...,'' Sarah said trying to explain her actions.

''Oh, we all know what you thought, but you were wrong,'' Adam said, not giving Sarah a chance to finish her sentence. "If you will excuse me.'' In outrage and disgust as he walked to his cabin.

''I am sorry James, but I need to fix this,'' Sarah said and ran after her husband.

James watched her run after Adam. He was left alone with his thoughts. Something strange had happened on this island. What if it didn't just happen to him? What if it had happened to everyone else? Before he could investigate this further, he had to make sure Jessica was OK, however terrible his conversation with her would be. He started his dreaded walk to Jessica's room and knocked on her door.

"Who is it?" she asked emotionally.

"It's me, please let me in," James replied nervously.

"Go away I have nothing say to you!"

"We need to talk," James pleaded, placing his right hand on the door.
"Haven't you done enough? Just leave me alone!" she yelled back.

"I know you are upset, and you have every right to be. I was wrong, please just give me a chance to explain myself," James pleaded.

"Why should I?"

"Because I need you in my life and I don't want to lose you," James begged in desperation.

Jessica remained quiet, struggling with the notion of letting James in. The silence was killing James, to him it meant the cards were stacked against him to ever regain her friendship again. He was suddenly jolted back to the moment by Jessica's response.

"It's open." she said. Without hesitation, James quickly opened the door and went in. He found Jessica sitting at the edge of the bed. She looked up as he came in, sadness written in her eyes.

"I am so sorry, I thought I was helping," James said.

"You had no right James, none whatsoever," Jessica said, standing up. "How could you?" She asked in exasperation at the whole situation. "I trusted you," she said sitting down again and lowering her face.

"Sarah would not listen to anything you and Adam had to say," James said, defending himself. Slowly he made his way to the bed. "I felt I had no choice," he continued, placing his hand on her shoulder. She kept quiet deliberating on everything he was saying and finally lifted her head.

"Couldn't you find another way?" she asked.

James looked her straight in the eye. Making absolutely sure she heard what he was about to say.

"She was accusing you of sleeping with her husband and I hated that. I respect you too much to let anyone speak like that to you." James kept silent waiting for a response, never losing eye contact.

Jessica's eyes showed the intense emotion she was experiencing at that moment. "What I shared with you; I don't go around telling people about. I told you because I thought I could trust you," she replied.

"You can," James protested.

Jessica laughed silently." I mean it," he insisted. The last thing James wanted was for his friend to lose faith in him. But the realization of what he had done was finally sinking in.
"I let you down. I get it. I had no right to tell them," he said, shaking his head. "I thought I was doing the right thing." Shame consuming him, all he could do was look away. "I messed up please forgive me." He turned his head back in her direction. A knock at the door startled them both.

"Who is it?" James yelled out.

"Anton, Sir." the steward of the ship replied. Jessica walked towards the door and opened it with a sad smile.

"Come in," she said. Jessica walked back to the bed and sat down.

The expression on both of their faces made it clear to Anton that they were in the middle of a very important discussion and they did not want to be disturbed. "Sorry for the interruption." Anton said, looking at both of them. "Regarding your last night on the yacht we will be having a bonfire on the island. The boat will be leaving for the island at six," Anton said without taking a breath.

Chapter 4

"Anton, I won't be joining the others on the island, I will be having dinner in my room tonight," Jessica replied. James was startled by her response.

"I need you to go with us tonight," he said under his breath, looking at her.

"Why?" Jessica whispered back at James in utter confusion.

"Please just say yes. I can't explain now," he spoke softly. Anton felt completely out place, as he watched the "discussion" between them.

"Fine I will go," Jessica whispered in frustration.

"Thanks, I owe you," he whispered back to her. Jessica discerned an embarrassed Anton looking at both of them.

"I will be joining the group for the bonfire after all," she said, feeling uneasy by the prospect of seeing Adam and Sarah after the entire debacle that happened between them earlier on.

"Please make sure that the Phillips join us," James asked Anton.

"Yes sir, if you will excuse me. I will be leaving now," Anton said as he briskly walked towards the door.

James quickly stood up, escorted him and let him out. He turned and found Jessica standing with her hands on her hips.

"OK we are alone. Are you going to tell me what's going on?'' she asked, quite annoyed with James.

"No, I will explain everything at the bonfire tonight,'' he said, while opening the door.

"You can't be serious!'' she shouted at him.

"I am deadly serious he said and quickly let himself out. He poked his head back in the door. 'Thank you for forgiving me," he said with a smile, and quickly shut the door before Jessica could utter another word.

The Price of Forgiveness

Sarah remained quiet watching her husband pretend to read a newspaper. Finally, unable to take his indifference anymore, she spoke. "Can we talk about this?'' she said, standing nervously in front of her husband.

"Nope,'' Adam replied bluntly from the sofa.

"Adam *please*."

Adam kept his silence while turning the page.

" I know you are not reading that damn thing!'' she cried out of frustration

Immediately Adam threw the paper to the floor and stood up, staring at her with raging eyes.

"You disgrace me and yourself, to our friends yelling like a mad woman and if you dare speak to me in that tone once again. I will walk out of this room right now!"

"Do you blame me?" she said in desperation. "I thought..." He stopped her from finishing her sentence.

"Yes, we all know what you thought." His reply was scornful, and he was outraged. "But I told you! You were wrong! Did you listen?" He added a hint of arrogance. Before Sarah could say anything else, their discussion was interrupted by a knock at the door.

"Who is it?" Adam yelled.

"Adam get a hold of yourself," she pleaded.

"Anton sir, may I come in?" he replied, alarmed by Adam's tone.

"Yes, come in Anton," Sarah replied.

Anton opened the door with a tense smile on his face. He quickly noticed the uneasiness between the two people standing in the room. He chose to brief and to the point.
"The boat will be leaving for the island in an hour for the bonfire dinner. Mr James is personally requesting your presence. I am sure you will be joining them,"

"Of course, we will be joining them. Thanks for letting us know Anton," Adam replied with a kinder tone, trying to diffuse the tension in the room.

"Yes sir," Anton replied. He sensed the need for the couple to be alone and decided to leave the room.

"If you will excuse me," he said as he walked out of the door.

Sarah was beside herself. "Adam, I don't think that's a good idea after what happened today. Can we just stay here please?"

"It will give you an opportunity to apologise," he said firmly as he sat back down.

"Well, I wanted her to simmer down before I tried talking to her again," Sarah said.

"I was not asking," Adam replied dismissively, while picking up his paper on the floor.

"Don't ask me to do this now. I just can't. I am just not ready to face her yet," Sarah pleaded with tears in her eyes.

"You will go to that bonfire, and you will apologise, end of discussion!" he barked out his instructions as he straightened his newspaper.

Chapter 4

"Adam be reasonable!"

"Be reasonable! "Adam looked up from his paper. "After what you've done, be reasonable!" He stood up and threw the newspaper on the floor again. "First you walk out on me and go exploring! Then you insult me and that kind woman who did nothing to deserve any of this!"

"I am so sorry; can you forgive me? I just lost it. It's this island, its playing with my mind. Please just tell me you forgive me," Sarah pleaded again and fell on her knees laying her head to her husband's knees. She could not stop crying.

Adam took hold of her shoulders and lifted her up to her feet.

"If you want my forgiveness you will go to that bonfire and you will apologise for you behaviour," Adam responded, holding on to her shoulders, and enjoying his dominant position. "Get ready we are leaving in an hour." He said it as he walked out of the room without looking back.

The drive to the beach was extremely uncomfortable. Sarah felt Adam's eyes staring at her throughout the boat drive, waiting for her to apologize to Jessica. It was a silent trip. Everybody was reliving their experiences on the island. None of
them had any idea what the others were thinking. None of them cared. Everybody was engrossed in their own thinking. The speed boat slowed down and stopped as they reached the shore. James was the first to notice that they had arrived.

"We are here," he said, holding Jessica's hand and helping her step off the boat. Adam watched him help her. Hand in hand Jessica and James walked to the buffet table. Unwilling but feeling obligated he carried his wife off the boat.

"Exactly when do you think you are going to apologize?" he asked sternly. He still held her in his arms yet there was nothing warm in his embrace. It felt cold and hard, his hands were gripping her tightly. He was angry and he wanted her to know it.

"Soon." she whispered, feeling afraid. "I just wanted us to reach the beach." Adam's grip became tighter. She felt the pain where he placed his hands under her arms and legs. "' Put me down," she cried out silently.

"Do it now," he said clenching his teeth and placed her on the ground. She nodded, walking in a hurry away from her husband and did not dare look back.

Jessica and James were still at the buffet table filling their plates with food as Sarah reached them.

"Jessica, can we talk for a minute?" Sarah asked, fidgeting, unable to look straight into Jessica's eyes for any length of time.

"I am eating," Jessica replied coldly.

"I am going to leave you two alone," James remarked. This time he was keeping himself out of the crossfire given what was about to begin. He looked around and saw his way out. "Adam is by the bonfire. He must be hungry I'll take him a plate." He filled another plate with food.

"No James that's not necessary," Jessica said annoyed.

"Oh yes, it is. Trust me," James said and kissed her on the cheek. Jessica kept quiet. Without saying anything else he walked towards the bonfire.

"I wanted to say I am sorry. I was way out of line," Sarah said nervously.

"You were," Jessica replied simply.

"It's not easy to say this but my husband is a serial cheater. Everybody knows. He is the talk of the town," Sarah said.

"Is there a point to this?" Jessica replied.

"When I saw the guilt in both your faces, I assumed you were sleeping with him," Sarah said.

"You assumed wrong," Jessica snapped.

"I know," Sarah replied. "I am so sorry."

Jessica kept silent and started to walk away.

Sarah wished the ground would open up and swallow her. She quickly grabbed Jessica's hand. "Please just put yourself in my shoes. I have been keeping this agony so deep inside me. Every day I am so unhappy, and I have to pretend I am happy when I am not. Yesterday I reached my breaking point. The thought of you with Adam.... I just lost it. I am really, really sorry and I am asking for your forgiveness," she said with tears streaming down her face like a waterfall that never stops falling.

As much as she didn't want to feel for the woman, Jessica could not help but have compassion for her. Sarah's tears touched her deeply. She understood how it felt to live in pain everyday of your life. To fight through the day, trying not to feel defeated or broken. Having no one to come to your aid until your body totally gives in. Wishing for death to end the dreaded life you live. She reached for Sarah and started to wipe her tears away.

"I understand how hard it must be for you. Living with a man like Adam," Jessica replied as she recalled Adams' failed attempt to seduce her. She pulled Sarah into an embrace.

"You have no idea, I feel so alone. Adam is being so difficult. He refuses to let me off the hook until I apologise to you. He is so furious with me, I don't think I can take the cold shoulder anymore. " Sarah said through her tears. She held on tightly to Jessica. It felt wonderful to have someone she could lean on. Jessica pulled back just enough to see Sarah's face.

"Still, it does not excuse your behaviour."

"I know" Sarah said as she wiped another tear from her face

. It was difficult for Jessica, not to choke up at this moment. Unable to control herself she allowed the tears to come. "I forgive you. Leave Adam to me. I will talk to him," she said smiling through the tears.

Sarah, relieved and grateful initiated the second embrace.

"Thank you Jessica," Sarah replied, smiling between tears, and eventually pulling back.

"Let's go and find the boys," Jessica answered while wiping one last tear from Sarah's eyes. Slowly the two women walked to the bonfire hand in hand ready to join the men. Without saying anything else to one other, they both knew they had just bonded in a way that would lead to a lifelong friendship.

The Bonfire

The sun had left for the day, leaving in its place the most beautiful glistening stars that draped the sky like a necklace drapes itself on a woman's neck line. The four of them were sitting around the bonfire. The peace between the two women caused the tension to disappear. Anton had driven back to the ship, giving them time to be alone.

"Sarah and I have buried the hatchet and I think it's time you two do the same. Everybody makes mistake. We are all guilty of one thing or another." Jessica remarked as she looked at Adam with condemning eyes.

Adams' haughtiness dissipated into thin air, he knew exactly what Jessica was implying with those condemning eyes as he turned to give a quick embrace to his wife.

Since the air was finally cleared within the group, this was the perfect time for James to do what he had wanted to do since they had arrived on the beach. He steeled himself and stood up.

"Guys, something happened to me on this island. Something incredible," he said. James could not stop trembling, every time he thought about what happened to him. The thought of discussing it with the others terrified him. Despite the fear, he pushed on. All eyes were on him.

"I could not sleep a couple of nights ago. I was restless and felt the need to take a walk at twelve midnight. Before I knew it, I was on the deck. I heard someone calling my name, but no one was around."

Everybody started fidgeting, as James looked around the bonfire. The blood leaving all their faces proved what he was suspecting. They all had been through the same experience, he concluded to himself. He became increasingly excited as he spoke.

"Suddenly I felt an overpowering aura take hold of me. It was astounding. Something I cannot explain," he said as he laughed shaking his head, still amazed by the whole experience.

"I thought it was God," Jessica said as she stood up.

James was surprised by what she was saying and quickly sat down. His eyes did not blink once as he listened to Jessica telling her story. "I still believe it was Him." She could not help but play with her hands. She was the one shaking like a leaf now. Jessica looked back at the faces that were watching her every move.

"It felt as if I was having a personal encounter with Him. I felt peacefulness beyond anything I have ever experienced. I felt Him pulling me, willing me to the sea. I had no control over myself and didn't want to have it. I would have done anything He told me to. I was compelled to look into the ocean and..."
She was interrupted. Sarah stood up, her face pale white from shock. For a while she could not say a word. Both women looked at each other lost for words. Both knew instinctively what had happened to the other.

"You were pulled to the bottom of the ocean," Sarah answered.

Still on her feet Jessica whispered, "Yes."

"I could breathe and walk under water," Sarah cut Jessica off from continuing with her story. "I was sure I had died." The excitement grew as she continued to speak. "I noticed a wooden birdhouse that captured my attention like nothing else ever did. Before I knew what was happening, I was looking through the window and saw.... I saw..." How could she say anything with Adam looking at her? What would he say? What would he do? She thought to herself. Bursting out in tears Sarah quickly sat down. Jessica's motherly instincts took over; taking her place next to her, she started to console her.

"She saw what she could never have. Something she has always wanted," Adam said as he began to rock back and forth, as he bent his knees. "You see your dream. Right there! Close enough to grasp it. Everything that can bring you the happiness you have always wanted," he said looking agitated. He felt as if he was losing his mind. He carried on speaking. "Suddenly all you want is that dream. You want to be part of it." Everybody felt Adam was exposing their inner most feelings at that moment. "And that damn house feels what you feel and drags you inside!" Adam screamed at the top of his lungs. Everyone became alarmed by his strong emotion. "If I didn't pull away, that thing would have sucked me in!" He quieted down as soon as he saw the concerned faces of the people watching him. "I was yanked out of the water and taken back to the deck," he concluded.

"So, we have all gone through the same experience," James said as he got to his feet.

"Yeah, no kidding, Sherlock," Adam mockingly replied.

"Look man I don't know what's bugging you but if you could let me finish," James replied.

"This island is what's bugging me! I just want to get out of here and pretend none of this ever happened!" Adam said in another outburst.

James ignored Adam's "meltdown" and continued speaking. "I think we have been given an opportunity by a higher power or God; I don't know. Jessica, you thought it was God, right?" Her response was a quick nod as she looked at him. She was speechless after everything she had heard. James continued, "I think we were chosen for a reason. Winning that competition was no accident.... I hope you will all forgive me, but I have to be frank to prove my point. All of us, are not happy with our lives...." All eyes were fixed on James. He knew he was walking on thin ice but resoluteness pushed him on. "When I was in that house, I saw myself singing on stage." A smile appeared on his face as if God had placed it there all by Himself. "An artist, living my dream." Slowly the smile evaporated from his face. "At home I have a pregnant woman I don't love, expecting me to marry her." James looked at Jessica and said, "We all know Jessica is celibate and a God-fearing woman." Jessica stared a hole through his heart!
"James, I didn't smack Sarah, but I will slap you," she said candidly. Sarah's face turned pink. James was unfazed. He continued speaking.

"Let's face it, there aren't many devout men who want to marry virgins."

"You are way out of line James," Jessica said steely.

"Just hear me out OK!" he said trying to calm Jessica down. "When you were in that house you saw yourself married to a principled man who didn't expect you to sleep with him before you married him, right?"

"Yes," she answered, feeling self-conscious.

"And back home a man is willing to marry you, but you have go to bed with him first, right?" he asked.

"Exactly what's your point James?" Jessica asked. She was starting to lose her composure.

"I am sorry, but I have to do this," James said and turned his attention to Sarah. "You saw Adam being faithful to you right?" Sarah gave a quick glance at her husband. Adams' face had turned blood red. He was furious.
Sarah replied in fear, "Yes," and immediately turned her face away.

James's attention was now on Adam. "Adam, you saw the same thing. Didn't you?"

"You have managed to offend everyone around you," Adam replied in disgust.

"I have a reason for that," James answered adamantly.

"Oh really?" Adam replied.

"My point is this. None of us are satisfied with our lives. So, what is keeping us here? I say we should all go back and enter the birdhouse," James said.

"You must be out of your mind!" Adam said furiously as he also stood up.

"This could be our chance of a life time!" James tenaciously replied

"Or it could be extra-terrestrials tricking us into entering their spaceship and doing experiments on us. Have you thought about that, Sherlock?" Adam asked seriously. Both of the women watched the two men continue with their argument leaving them dumbfounded.

"Oh, come on Adam that's crazy!" James replied.

"Everything about this island is crazy! It could be a trap!" Adam said vehemently.

"Adam this is my chance, and I am not going to let you take it from me!"

"If you want to be a study for some alien, please be my guest but don't involve us. You do it on your own! Leave us out of it!" Adam sarcastically answered back.

James felt like he was about to explode "Are you afraid that Sarah will leave the fornicator you have become and find a self-respecting man in that birdhouse?" James asked out of spite.

"You pig!" Adam screamed, flinging himself at James. The two men fell to the ground and started hurling punches at one another. Both of the women screamed as they watched the altercation between the two men.
"Stop. Stop. Stop," they called out to no avail. James was on top of Adam, hurling one punch after the other regardless of Adam's well-built physical structure!

Fearful for her husband, Sarah called out to Jessica. "We have to do something!" Jessica threw herself at James and held on tightly not knowing what else to do.

"Get off me!" James yelled as he tried to push her off him.

"No!" Jessica shouted.

Sarah dissolved into tears once again, unable to do anything else but helplessly watch her husband being attacked. "James! Stop! You're hurting him," Sarah cried out.

Jessica held on tighter and tighter to James as he struggled to get her off his back. "Please James, I am begging you,"

James finally relented, unable to do any more damage on Adam's face with Jessica on his back. Jessica exhaled, out of relief. She untangled herself from him and helped James to his feet. Both men had blood and bruises on their faces, especially Adam, their clothes torn and covered with sand.

"Fine let's put it to a vote," James said out of breath while looking at the women. Sarah was by her husband's side wiping the blood on his nose with a tissue she found in her pocket. Adam did not have the strength to stand up. The women were rattled to say the least.

"James is right, we should all vote," Jessica replied. Sarah gave a quick nod, frightened out of her wits.

 "Wait," Adam said out of breath. "I want to say something first." "What?" James asked. He was starting to get agitated again.

"You had your chance to talk, now it's my turn!" Adam answered as he tried to get on his feet. Sarah quickly helped him up being the dutiful wife she was. "Our lives may not count for much," Adam said. He was out of breath dripping blood from his nose and mouth. He looked broken and discouraged. "We breathe in the filthy stink of disappointment every day and we almost suffocate from it." His eyes had lost all the fire that had been there a second ago. "We have been kicked in the stomach so much by this world that we have lost all sense of feeling. But we are used to it, we can handle it. We don't know the level of suffering and despair that's waiting for us out there, under that ocean. What if it's more than we can take? Life has never been good to any of us. Why should it start now?" Everybody was listening intently as he spoke. "I say grin and bear what we are used to," Adam painfully continued as he looked at his wife and Jessica.

"We don't have to. That's the point," James remarked out of frustration.

"Are you going to let me finish?" Adam asked. James kept quiet, looking at Adam in anger. "I know I don't want to get my hopes up, only to be let down again," Adam sadly continued. "Going out there could be the worst decision we make in our lives," he said while pointing to the water. "We don't know what's out there. I say we all go home. That's all I have to say," he said as he sat down. He felt completely depleted.

Before James could say anything, Jessica started speaking. "Adam is right," she said.

"What! You too?" James replied. He looked at Jessica in disbelief.

"James, if a part of you didn't believe what Adam is saying is true, you would leave us behind," she continued. James fell silent. "You are just as scared as the rest of us," James nodded in shame, feeling completely exposed "We all could be making a mistake by going into that water. I know you feel betrayed by me right now, but I have my reasons'," She said strongly. James remained silent and allowed her to speak.
"I could have had a lifetime with a man who treated me like gold, but I made the wrong choice, I trusted what my heart was feeling.... We all know how falling in love for the first time can do to you. It's

so intense like the tide, tossing you around with no chance of escaping. I was still in love with my first love Kevin, when Caleb and I started seeing each other. Anyway, Kevin wanted me back and naturally I took him back. I was only eighteen, so naive. I ended things with Caleb and left him with a broken heart," she said, her eyes full of regret. "I truly believed that what I and Kevin had was the real thing." Tears started swirling up in her eyes. "How untrue that was. As soon as Caleb was out of the picture, Kevin started messing around again, making me feel like a fool and unloved. I had to leave him. I was twenty-two when I accepted Jesus Christ into my life, He taught me many things. I learnt about, self-love, self-respect and how a man treats the woman he loves,'' she said with conviction. What I shared with Kevin was one sided, the love was not returned. Caleb loved me and he was not afraid to show it. I didn't have to wonder. His actions sang his love for me every day. ''I realized that he was everything I ever wanted in a man and so much more when I found Christ !'' she said, her eyes still full of the love she had lost. "My heart belonged to Caleb since that day.'' Jessica gave a half smile. "He married someone else before I could tell him. I was devastated and I promised myself to never make that same mistake ever again," she said, her determination written all over her face. "Following our emotions can be our downfall! That birdhouse is using our feelings to get to us. Let's not allow it,'' she asked earnestly, as she looked at the faces that were watching her intently. "I am done trusting my feelings," she said regretfully. "Someone wants to marry me. I have to go all the way with him first and I hate that, but I won't be alone anymore. At least I will have someone to hold me at night." For a while everybody kept silent, they were all touched by everything she said and were deeply sad for her.

Sarah slowly stood up. "I have something to say too." Her eyes were full of emotion. She burst into tears as she looked at her husband's eyes. Adam had never looked so demoralized and run down, in all the years she was married to him, she thought to herself. "It's hard to give up on your dream, especially if it's in your grasp," she said through her tears. "My life is nothing but a joke for everyone to gossip about, but I know I won't be able to raise my hopes up only to have them crushed again. My heart won't take it." She choked up. "I say we go home to what we know and understand." She said that with conviction. The silence took over. Everything that needed to be said was spoken. James knew it was pointless he did not have a chance in hell to convince them to take the opportunity that was being offered as he started with the voting process.

"Everyone in favour of going back under water, raise your hand." He was the only one who lifted his arm. He continued in exasperation, "Everyone in favour of going home and never discussing this again, raise your hand."

Adam's hand was the first to come up. "James you are just a jerk who made a girl pregnant, now you are trying to run from your responsibilities," he said cruelly.

"It takes one to know one," James cutely replied. Adam remained silent and gritted his teeth. Sarah raised her hand as well. Jessica finally put her hand up. She could not bear to look at James in the face.

James looked at the arms raised up in the air and felt betrayed by his so-called friends. Everyone walked silently towards the speedboat, coming back to fetch them. It was taking them back to the ship for one last night. The friendships they had formed with one another were gone the moment they raised their hands and voted. Too much of whom they were as individuals was unmasked. Life had taught them to hide the truth from society and especially from themselves, society had taught them to always put on a show, always pretend everything was perfect when it wasn't.

Chapter 5

Going Home

*T*he four passengers had no memory of boarding the plane or driving to the airport. Their last memory was being on the speedboat, taking them back to the beach. They woke up from a deep slumber and discovered they were back on the plane flying home. The flight back home was different and morbid. You didn't hear laughter or champagne glasses clinking to a toast. Everybody sat in separate seats, including Adam and Sarah. It didn't come as a surprise to anyone when they walked to their different limos waiting to take them back to their houses, that no one said goodbye. No one wanted to have anything to do with the other ever again.

The Proposal

Jessica was completely surprised to find her apartment filled with red roses. There were vases with roses all over the place. She threw her heavy suitcase on her bed and began to undress but quickly stopped when she heard a man's voice.

"Surprise!" It was Derrick holding one white rose standing against the bathroom door.

"Derrick!" she screamed. "You startled me," she said buttoning her blouse up.

"So, I see. I should have hidden little a while longer," he teased.

"Don't be silly," she blushed. "How is your leg?" she asked with concern.

"I don't need crutches anymore, I am perfectly fine," he replied.

"I am so glad to hear that," she said with a smile.

"My darling it's time to be serious," he said and extended his right arm long enough for Jessica to notice the diamond engagement ring on top of the rose.

Chapter 5

"I don't know what to say," she gasped. Jessica was completely blind-sided; she didn't expect a romantic proposal. In fact, quite the contrary; she expected a lashing for leaving. She thought to herself.

Say yes. Derrick said as he walked towards her with all the charm he could muster. Jessica stumbled back and fell on the edge of the bed. As she sat up Derrick had reached the bed and was on one knee.

"I thought you were angry with me," she said, trying to absorb what was happening!

"Absence makes the heart grow fonder. All is forgiven," he said while placing the ring on her left finger, without waiting for a response. Derrick gave Jessica his smooth confident pompous smile as he kissed her hand.

"So, Sweetness, what is your answer?" he asked with a smug grin on his face.

"Yes, I will marry you Derick," she said, trying not to feel like a sell-out, as she conjured a grateful smile.

"Of course, you will," he said as he stood up and sat next to her. "So, I have another surprise for you," he said, feeling so pleased with himself. "We are getting married tomorrow.

"What!" Jessica gasped. She was sure she hadn't heard him clearly. "Could you say that again?" she asked in complete shock.

"While you were away Donna and I have been planning our wedding," he said grinning from ear to ear. "That was our agreement, right?" he said. In Derrick's mind, this was a rhetorical question. He made sure Jessica understood that, with the hard tone of his voice.

"Of course," she sheepishly replied. I would have liked to plan my own wedding, but I guess this is his way of showing that he cares, she tried to convince herself. Derrick noticed the sad look on her face.

"Don't hold back your excitement on my account," he said ironically.

"I am sorry," she answered. "I have always wanted to plan my own wedding, but..." She didn't have the chance to finish her sentence because Derrick interrupted her.

"You know Jessica; I didn't expect this from you. You should be thankful that I even want to marry you," he said, his arrogance had no bounds. "Which means tonight, you and I are making love." Jessica gulped. "Remember you're not getting any younger. Didn't you turn thirty-one this year?" he said harshly. Derrick had a razor-sharp knife for a tongue a lot of the time. As usual he knew exactly what to say to cut Jessica to the very core of her heart. Her face was drawn, and she looked flushed.

"Forgive me Derrick. I guess I am still overwhelmed by the whole thing. I am really grateful and happy for everything," she awkwardly replied.

Chapter 5

"That's more like it...Alright then I will leave you to rest," he said while standing up from the bed.

"You are leaving?'' she asked.

"Yes, dear I have things to do besides fawning over you. Its eleven o'clock in the morning and I have a practice to run. Our wedding won't pay for itself," Jessica could never say or do anything right in Derrick's mind. He spent his spare time playing his favourite game, hurting her feelings. One way or the other she always managed to fall under that sharp tongue of his. He really enjoyed making her feel small.

"I didn't mean to imply you had nothing better to do. I am sorry," she said. Jessica wanted to get under a rock and hide.

"So, I will see you tonight at my place at eight. Don't be late," he said and kissed her on the cheek. She bobbled her head and gave him her best pretend happy smile.

"Thank you for the roses," she said as she watched him walk out of her room.

"You're welcome, Sweetness," he replied as he gave her a quick glance and left.

Jessica let out a long sigh and did what came naturally to her, when she was bothered by something. She started speaking to herself. "Alone at last. He can be so patronising. "Sweetness" He knows how

148

much I despise it, when he calls me that. I have been home for less than an hour and I am already in a whirlwind! I am coming back from a strange island, only to find Derrick at my place with a ring! Expecting me to sleep with him tonight! Not to mention having a wedding tomorrow! Can my life be more insane?" She moaned.

Her ramblings were suddenly interrupted by her answering machine beeping. She had a message. She quickly ran to the lounge, hoping with all her might it was Donna. She desperately needed to talk to a friend right now! she thought. She quickly pressed the button on her machine.

"Hello Jessica," she heard a woman's voice coming from the speaker. The voice sounded slightly familiar. "Do you know who this is?" the voice said with a giggle. "You do, don't you?" It was a rhetorical question.

The voice sounds just like me, but I can't be sure, she said to herself. Finally, the pin dropped, and it dawned on her that the voice coming out of the speaker phone was hers! I sound so happy and confident, Jessica thought to herself. The jubilance and contentment could be felt in each and every word she heard coming from her answering machine.

"Your husband is waiting for you," she heard the voice say. Jessica didn't know what to say or think after hearing that sentence. My what!? she said to herself, her eyes wide open. She was past shock or surprise! Nothing could describe what she was feeling at this moment! She felt as if she was losing her mind.

"Come back to the island," the voice proceeded to say. "God didn't forget about you. A limo will pick you up tomorrow at six thirty in the morning and take you back to the island," the voice continued. Jessica waited to see if the voice would say anything else, but the speaker phone went completely off. She could feel every fibre of her being shaking. She could not move an inch. The only thing she was able to do was look at her answering machine in awe!

The Invitation: James

"It's about time you got back! Your girl has been calling this house nonstop! Asking me where you went. Didn't you tell her you were going on holiday?" Those were the welcoming words James heard from his father standing in the passage as James entered his home.

"I was so excited about the trip I completely forgot to tell her I was leaving!" James said as he dropped his bags on the floor.

"That's no way to start a marriage," Reginald said.

"We are not married yet Dad," James replied. His father gave him a stern look that told him to watch his mouth.

"I am sorry Dad I didn't mean to be rude," James humbly apologized. "How have you been? How is the vet going?" James asked trying to lighten the mood a little.
Reginald would not budge. "It's fine," he replied gruffly. "Listen, she called again yesterday. She wants to see you tonight at eight at her parent's house," he continued.

"OK I will go and apologize," James replied. He felt as if someone was tightening a rope around his neck.

"Good, I am going to work," his father said as he opened the door.

"Alright I will see you when you get back," James answered with a tense smile on his face.

"You are not coming to work?" Reginald asked irritated.

"Dad, I just got back!" James frankly replied, shocked by his father's insensitivity.

"You're the laziest boy! If I ever saw one!" his father said in anger. Both men started raising their voices.

"Dad it was a long flight!" James defensively replied.

"Save me your excuses! Just be at work tomorrow. Eight sharp and don't be late!" Reginald ordered, as he slammed the door behind him.

James picked his bags up and started walking to his bedroom but was stopped right in his tracks as he heard his voice coming out of the speaker phone. The answering machine had turned itself on supernaturally!

"Hey man come back to the island," he heard his own voice talking to him from the machine. James dropped his bags on the floor, he was completely stunned by what he was hearing. "You know you want to," his voice teased. "Mom wanted you to be happy. Now you can be." James was amazed by the determination and confidence his voice had as he listened to himself carry on speaking. "She did not let you down. God heard her prayers," the voice spoke with compassion and love. James could feel the tears stinging his eyes. God heard Mom's prayers, he thought to himself, wiping them from his face.

"A limo will be waiting outside the house at six thirty tomorrow morning to take you to the airport," the voice continued. "James, Mom is so proud of the man you are going to become. Well done my man. Congratulations on your dreams coming true." James had joyousness and a feeling of fulfilment in his voice as he listened to the machine. The answering machine turned back into a mute object after that. James ran out of the door, pushing his legs as fast as they could carry him, leaping and jumping dustbins, running through a green light, and trying to avoid being knocked down by cars, determined not to stop. He ran to Jessica's house.

The Invitation: Sarah and Adam

Adam opened the door of their "loving home." He walked straight to their bedroom and dropped the bags on the floor. Coming back from the bedroom he found Sarah standing in the middle of the living room staring at the furniture. Sarah began to remember the tears she cried in that house. Every room had memories of Adam rejecting her and her heart torn apart. She stared long and hard at the beige couch she cried herself to sleep on, the nights Adam didn't come home.

Irritated by his wife staring into space Adam yelled "What are you doing?"

Sarah was embarrassed, she was caught daydreaming. She quickly replied "Nothing," and swiftly walked to the kitchen, intent on keeping busy. "Do you want something to eat?" she asked as she put her apron on.

"Not hungry," he replied abruptly.

"Coffee? I am making a cup for myself."

"Actually, I am going down to the pub," he answered as he walked towards the door.

"Back to our routine I see," Sarah mumbled. She made sure Adam couldn't hear what she was saying.

As He was about to walk out of the door, the answering machine came on. When he heard himself speaking on the answering machine, he turned, fell backwards, and landed on the couch.

"Come back to the island." The voice sounded just like Adam's, Sarah thought to herself. She looked at her husband in amazement. "Is this supposed to be a joke?" she asked.

"I swear Sarah I had nothing to do with this!" he replied shocked by what he just heard and by what Sarah was suspecting. "Why are you blaming me?" he asked aggravated.

"What am I supposed to think? Your voice is on our machine!" Sarah shouted.

"It's not me!" Adam defensively yelled back.

"It sounds like you!" Sarah screamed.

"Are you two pointing fingers at each other?" the voice on the speaker phone teasingly asked. This time it was a woman's voice speaking and she sounded exactly like Sarah.

"Now how do you explain that!" Adam accusingly yelled back.

"Shh!" Sarah abruptly replied, waving her hands in an attempt to keep her husband quiet. "She is still talking."
Adam said nothing else but listened to the voice.
"I bet Adam you think Sarah is playing a sick joke on you now?" His voice again on the answering machine. He could not believe what he was hearing. His eyes were wide open as he looked at his wife.
"And Sarah, I know you are thinking the
same thing about Adam." Her voice was now the one poking fun at them. Sarah walked quietly to the couch and sat beside Adam. She could not believe what she was hearing! She was sure she would lose her mind any moment as she stared back at her husband's astonished face. It was clear to Adam and Sarah that another version of themselves had left a message on their answering machine, each giving the other an opportunity to speak.

Both of their voices sounded happy and playful. The voices enjoyed teasing the shocked couple, as they listened to their answering machine.

"Listen this is not a joke. It is real. We are you," Adam's voice on the speaker phone replied.

"Come back to the island. I promise you won't regret it. You can still have the life you both wanted. It's not too late Sarah," her voice on the speaker phone said. It took everything in her not to burst out and cry as soon as she heard that.

"It's never too late with God," Adam's voice said in the machine.

"What!" Adam yelled. Nothing could have shocked him more, than to hear himself speak about God!

"Yes Adam, I said God, and soon you will believe too," his voice on the speaker phone said. "A limo will be waiting outside, to take you back to the airport at six thirty in the morning," Sarah's' voice on the speaker spoke. The couple listened attentively, expecting to hear more, but instead they heard the answering machine supernaturally turn itself off.

They heard a loud knock on their door and heard James's voice. "Adam. Open up!" Sarah was surprised to find Jessica standing next to James as she opened the door.

"Come in," she said and smiled as she let them in.

"I know it happened to both of you, so please don't even try to deny it!" James said pointedly. He was a man on a mission. The spark in his eyes could have burned an entire forest. There was a passion and determination in him, that nothing could quench. Sarah sat quietly next to her husband. She had never seen James this excited before. He started pacing up and down the lounge frantically.

"I know you received a message from yourselves, telling you to come back to the island. It happened to Jessica and me, and I know it happened to you too!" said James.

"He ran all the way to my place and confronted me. He insisted we come here," Jessica said in amazement and sat next to Sarah.

"How did you know where she stayed?" Adam asked accusingly.

"Who cares how I got there! I asked both of you a question!" James shouted, his annoyance escalating. Adam was about to yell something back at James, but Jessica quickly spoke.
"We exchanged addresses on the plane on our way to the island," she politely explained, trying to keep the two men from fighting again.

"How did you know where to find us?" Adam asked Jessica.

"I gave Jessica my address on the island too," Sarah responded while looking at James, who was still pacing around her lounge. James looked as if he was about to burst a vein.

"Now that we have all that straightened out can somebody answer my question?" James asked.

"You don't come into my house and start making demands, yelling like a mad man!" Adam shouted at James. The two men started walking towards each other.

"You listen here!" James responded aggressively.
Sarah quickly stood up and screamed. "It's true it happened to us too!" She immediately felt bad for speaking, as she stared into her husband's angry eyes, but she knew it was the only way to keep them from fighting again. "We were just listening to the message," she said as she sat down.

"Thank you, Sarah. You should all know that I am going back," James confidently announced.

"It's aliens tricking us to go back, and you are falling into their trap!" Adam yelled indignantly as he stood up.

"I really don't care what you think!" James hollered back, his eyes blazing with fire as he pointed his finger at Adam.

"You would risk being tortured for the rest of your life! For what?" Adam shouted at James.

"Every day is torture for me!" James blurted out. Everyone was astonished by his outburst, but the inferno burning deep inside him quickly subsided. No one said a word, not even Adam. Adam sat next to his wife and waited for James to speak. They all waited for him to explain himself. James slowly spoke and revealed the sadness he hid from the world; tears began to form in his eyes. "Excruciating torture, and it never ends. If it turns out to be aliens in that ocean, the only difference is I will be experiencing physical pain instead of emotional torment. So, what is the difference? One way or the other I will be in agony. If I have to choose the kind of hurt I have to bear, I choose the aliens. My body will give in from the pain eventually, but if I stay here, I can never escape this misery. I will waste away, waiting to die. I can't do that, and I won't do that!" he said with a ferocious look in his eyes. He stood up with assurance. "I came here to tell all of you that I am leaving tomorrow. You can all stay here if you want to, but I am leaving!"

"Well James, if you want to kill yourself then go ahead and do it, we are staying right here," Adam said.

"Does Adam speak for everyone in this room?" James asked, keeping his eyes straight at Jessica.
"It's my wedding tomorrow. I am meeting Derrick at his place tonight," Jessica hesitantly replied.

"You are going to sleep with him?" James was indignant. Jessica could not bear to look at him another moment. She quickly looked down at the carpeted floor.

"That's the agreement," she said softy.

"Why are you selling yourself short when you can have the real thing?" James asked with a worried look on his face.

"I told you why," she defensively replied as she raised her head. "I just can't risk making the wrong decision again. This is safer," she answered sadly. Adam and Sarah kept quiet and listened to the two friends arguing.

"You are so afraid of making a mistake again, that you can't even see how you are making one right now," he replied disapprovingly. The defeat and shame on her face said it all.
'It's her choice to make, James," Adam butted in. He looked sternly at James.

"Of course, you would say that." James said to Adam. His disgust for the other man was quite clear. He let out a small laugh and looked at Sarah, then at Adam and looked back at Sarah again. Sarah looked like a deer in headlights. She did not want to hear what James was about to say.

"What about you Sarah, do you feel the same way?" James asked with a sly smile on his face.

"I... I... I...," Sarah started.

"Why do I bother asking you? You allow Adam to dictate your life. Tell me Sarah, do you ever think for yourself?" Sarah blushed. She could not say a thing, mortified by what James had said. Before

159

anyone could stop him, Adam stood up and punched James on the face. James did not retaliate. He knew he deserved it.

"I want you out of my house or I will throw you out!' Adam yelled in anger.

"Don't bother, I am leaving. I have said my piece. I am taking the chance that has been given to me and nothing is going to stop me," James fearlessly replied as he wiped the blood on his nose.

Adam wanted to tear him to pieces. He seethed, "I am not going to tell you again." Jessica knew she had to get James out of the house before both men started fighting again. She immediately grabbed James' hand and they walked out.

Adam slammed the door behind them and was surprised by the expression on his wife's face, as he turned back and faced her. Sarah stood up and stared at Adam for a very long time then silently walked to their bedroom. She locked the door behind her and stayed in that room for the whole afternoon.

The Car Ride

Jessica drove to James' house in silence. She was upset with him.

"Thank you for taking me home," he said, looking at her.

Forced to break the silent treatment she was giving him, she replied, "Well I was not going to let you walk all the way home. I still can't believe what you did to Sarah."

James looked straight ahead and did not say a word. Jessica's irritation was beginning to escalate by the second on account of his attitude. "Don't you feel guilty at all?" she asked coldly.

Turning to face Jessica he calmly said, "As a matter of fact I don't. It had to be done," and then he looked straight ahead.

Jessica was at the end of her tether. "You run all the way to my place, start a fight with Adam and break poor Sarah's heart! James what's happening to you!?"

"If you really want to know then stop the car," he said adamantly.

Jessica quickly turned into a nearby parking lot and switched the ignition off. She looked straight into his eyes and said, "I am listening."

James was composed and courageous, looking so audacious and comfortable with himself in a way he had never been before. He looked as if he was coming into his own, Jessica reflected as she looked into his eyes.

"I just can't hold back anything anymore. The island has changed me. I fight for what is right," he said with certainty, Jessica could not help but gain respect for him. "I don't hide how I feel. I am not the same James who allowed people to walk all over him. When I received that call from myself, something was triggered in me that can't be stopped." A part of her was in awe of the "new James." She didn't feel an ounce of irritation at him anymore. She was envious of who James was becoming.

"I admire everything you are saying James, but does it have to involve hurting people in the process?" she asked.

"Yes, even if it means I have to hurt *your* feelings," he said as he stared long and hard at Jessica.

"We are not talking about me," she said in a feisty manner.

"Well, we are now."

"James, you have said enough, and I don't want to argue with you." "Who is arguing? All I want to do is talk," he replied honestly with a smile.

"You're not going to let this go?" she asked in exasperation.

"Nope," he continued to smile.

She could not help but grin, James knew which buttons to press to get her defences down. He was truly like a brother to her, she thought to herself.

"OK let's talk," she replied. The smile faded away from James' face. He knew this was the only chance he had to get through to Jessica. It was time to get serious he concluded.

"I know you think you are playing it safe with Derrick," he said.

"I am why you can't see that?"

"Don't you know that playing it safe is the most dangerous thing someone like you can do?" James answered with concern.

"Someone like me?" she asked in confusion.

"You have passion and dreams; I see it in your eyes. If you settle, that twinkle will slowly burn out," he said fervently.

"Thank you for your concern, but I am a grown woman. I can take care of myself," she said firmly. James started to shake his head disapprovingly. Jessica was determined to make him understand. "James, I lost something good, something wonderful because I trusted my feelings. This is my chance to fix my mistake,"

"Caleb," he said.

"Yes, Caleb, who else?" she replied miserably

"Has it ever occurred to you that Caleb was never meant for you?" he asked trying to be as humane as possible.

"What! No," she said raising her voice, then annoyed at herself, "I did this, I made the wrong choice."

"If he was meant for you, why didn't you meet him first?" James asked her directly. He blindsided her with his question. It was so unexpected she didn't know what to say. "Caleb could have been your first love. You could have met him first, instead of Kevin. God could have made sure of that. Why didn't he?" he asked in a straightforward tone. All these questions were starting to give her a headache, she thought to herself, forcing her to face facts she had been trying to avoid all her life.

"Are you blaming God for this?" she asked.

"No, I am trying to open your eyes to the truth...You met Kevin first and fell deeply in love. How was that your fault?" he asked gently.

"I.... I... don't know," she answered, her voice breaking. James knew she was about to cry. He tried to be as affectionate as he possibly could as he continued. Leaning towards her, he took her hand, "Caleb could have waited for you if he was meant for you, no matter how long it took, but he didn't, he got married,"

"Yes, but that's because I kept pushing him away. It took years to get over Kevin," she said with tears in her eyes.

"You two could have met and fallen in love right after you had found God," he wiped her tears away with his finger. "As soon as you realized what love was really about, why didn't you?" he delicately asked. James looked straight into her teary eyes. He didn't flinch but waited for an answer.

"Why are you doing this to me?" she sobbed.

"To keep you from making the biggest mistake of your life," he lovingly replied. She could not face him anymore and looked down. James held her shoulders, forcing her to look at him. "You followed your heart. You thought Kevin was the one, there is no sin in that," he said carefully. "You did nothing wrong. How were you supposed to know it would never last with Kevin?" he sincerely asked and with compassion, he continued, "You were only eighteen." The tears kept coming as she listened to James carrying on. "Why are you punishing yourself for something you had no control over?" he asked.

"Because I lost Caleb," she cried out. "How can I ever forgive myself?" She sobbed dissolving into tears. James held her close and whispered in her ear.

"There is nothing to forgive."
"I lost Caleb, James... I lost Caleb!" Jessica cried out, and hysterically cried on his shirt. She now felt like she had never loved anyone like that, not even Kevin. It was as if she and Caleb were one person. Without Caleb her heart stopped working, like a clock that stopped ticking.

"He was never meant for you." James said softly.

"Stop saying that!" she said pushing him away.

James could see her pain, but he knew that in order to help her, he had to hurt her. "He was not meant for you. He was meant for someone else."

"How can that be?" she cried out. "He loved me, the way I always wanted a man to love me," she said as she bitterly continued to weep. James could not help but reach out for her and hug her again.

"Maybe God was using him to teach you about love. The real kind, so that when the right one comes along, you don't mess it up." He brushed her back, trying to console her. "Be grateful that you knew him and that he loved you once, the way you deserve to be loved. It's time you let him go."

"I can't," she sobbed into his shirt and clung to him. "How do you let go of something that fits so perfectly with you?" she asked between tears.

"If you and Caleb fit so perfectly together then why is he married to someone else? Why didn't he wait until you came back to him?" "I don't know," she said as she choked up.

"Yes, you do," he insisted while rubbing the back of her head. "He fits with someone else Jessica, not you. It's time to face facts. Look to the present and the future. Forget the past," he pleaded. James held on to her shoulders and forced her to look at him again. "Derrick is the wrong guy for you. The man in that birdhouse is the man you should be with. A man that loves you for everything you are, the way Caleb did and so much more," he said with such conviction.

"I can't James," Jessica said as she burst into fresh tears.

"What is keeping you from taking this chance?" he asked, deep concern written all over his face.

"It's just too good to be true," she said as she wiped the tears from her face.

"So what? I say we take this gift and don't ask why" James said decisively. This was wisdom, James's style.

"I don't think I have the courage to believe in my dreams any more or even fight for them. It's been too long, and I have had too many disappointments, to not think that there is something wrong with this picture. It's time to give up!" she cried out desperately.

"Never give up on your dreams. Fight for them. Do whatever it takes," James passionately replied as he looked deep into her eyes. "I am not like you James."

"I think you are," he said with a straightforward tone.

"Whatever, James," she said mockingly. Her eyes looked blank and drained. "It's getting late; Derrick will be waiting for me." She turned the ignition and started driving again.

Chapter 5

"We are not done talking," James said.

"Yes, we are! I am done talking about this, so can we please just drop it!" She teared up again. Her face full of emotion, proved what James was thinking as he looked at her. He knew it was a lost cause to try and persuade her to go with him. Too much had happened to her for her to believe in the island, he reflected.

They both went silent for a long while. When they had nearly reached James' house he said despondently, "I thought I had reached you back there. This can't be what you wanted for yourself." His face was full of brotherly love and concern. Jessica kept silent and switched off the ignition. She knew this would be the last time she would ever see him again. It took everything in her power not to burst out and cry again. She wanted to hold on to him and never let go, but she knew she had to be stoic if she was going to get him out of her car. James stepped out of the vehicle feeling like a failure. Jessica started the ignition again and yelled out "I will never forget you," and drove away.

Her Choice

Sarah came out of her room as the sun was setting. She looked at her husband drinking his coffee in the kitchen. She slowly walked to the kitchen and sat across the table.

"I was wondering when you were going to come out of that room," Adam remarked.

"I needed some time out to think," she said.

"Thinking about what James said right?" he asked in an arrogant tone.

"Among other things."

"Like what?"

"Me leaving you," she calmly replied.

Adam's face started turning pale from shock. He tried to absorb what his wife was saying, but to no avail. He could not even construct a single sentence at this point. Pulling himself from his chair he slowly stood up.

"What did you just say?" he asked in disbelief.

Looking him straight in the eye she stood up and said, "I said I am leaving you Adam; I am going to the island with James."
Adam's face turned from pale to red and to fury.
"Have you lost your damn mind?" he screamed from the top of his lungs. Sarah was like a new woman, strong and composed unmoved by his antics.

"I have never been clearer about what I want in my whole life. I am perfectly sane, and I am leaving you. You can join me or stay here but either way I am going," she undauntedly replied. Adam could not believe what he was hearing. What shocked him the most was the intense single-mindedness in his wife's eyes. Immediately his anger started to rise from the pit of his stomach.

"Did you forget about the aliens?" he shouted.

"We don't know what is out there," she said without flinching and folded her arms. His yelling was not affecting her at all.

"My point exactly! We don't know what's out there!" he bellowed in frustration.

"There is a strong possibility that the faithful man I fell in love with and married is on that island, and I am willing to risk my life to get him back."

Adam could not say anything for a second, his anger was replaced with shame. Sarah sat back down and waited for Adam to speak again.

"We have discussed this before. I thought you and I were on the same page when it comes to our marriage. You have been such a trooper all these years and I ..." Sarah interrupted him while he was speaking.

Standing quickly back up again she said, "I don't want to be a trooper anymore!" Adam calling her a trooper once again stoked the hidden pain she had been keeping all these years. "I stayed because I had no choice. I could not leave you because I loved you so much. I could not bear to live without you, even if staying with you killed me every day inside. But for the first time in my life, I have the power and strength to leave," she said sternly. "I want to be with someone who loves me and who wants to touch me. A man who is loyal to me. A man who does not run after every skirt he sees. A man who is in the house long enough to give me children," she said firmly.

Adam felt as if Sarah had kicked him right at the pit of his stomach. He could not say another word. The ground was collapsing right under his feet. He could not help but sit slowly down. Sarah could not stand her husband at this moment, standing near to Adam was too awkward. She needed to create some distance. She walked towards the kitchen wall and leaned back.

"Nothing you say or do is going to change my mind, Adam. I am going to that island," she said coolly.

Adam finally found his words again. "This is about what James said.... about you right?"
"What James said really made me think," she said while pointing to the direction of her bedroom. "I took a long, hard look at myself and I didn't like what I saw," she said. "I have allowed you to sentence us to a life of unhappiness. You have made me accept things about you which no woman should ever have to accept about her husband. You served it up in a cold dish and I ate it up for years like the good little wife I was. I was trapped. Well not anymore. I am free from you and this marriage, and I am never coming back," she said without any emotion.

171

Chapter 5

"You're leaving me Sarah?" he asked out of hopelessness, feeling his heart ripping to pieces. The tears started to rain down Adam's face.

"Why are you so shocked?" she asked in a placid manner. "Isn't this, what you wanted? Isn't this, what you have been pushing me to do all these years?" she asked her husband, unmoved by his tears. The compassionate Sarah, who cared more about other people's feelings than herself had been replaced by a strong woman. A woman who would not care for others at the cost of hurting herself.

"You're leaving, and now that it is happening, I cannot imagine living my life without you. With you here, I have the strength to accept this unsatisfying life. I cannot do this without you," he cried.

"Then come with me," Sarah said. Her steel cold stare was now replaced with a glimmer of hope in her eyes.

"I can't," Adam replied decisively.

"You mean you won't," Sarah said with all the hope dripping away from her eyes.

"I mean I can't," he responded defensively. "And you can't go if I stay. You need me to create your happily ever after, remember?"

"No, I don't," Sarah answered matter-of-factly. "When I had that vision of us in that birdhouse, you were nowhere in sight. You were back in the cabin sleeping. When I go to that island another Adam will be waiting for me, while you remain here. I am sure of it. We were pulled under water, inside a tiny birdhouse and survived. Are you trying to tell me as powerful as that island is, it cannot create another you? Please don't make me laugh Adam."

He wanted the earth to open up at that instance and swallow him up. Adam's face could not hide his humiliation. He felt so small, not like a man at all.

Determined not to lose his wife Adam tried again. "What if its aliens and they torture you all your life?" he asked.

"Doesn't matter," she candidly replied. "I know torture. I can take torture. This marriage is torture for me so if you are trying to save me from pain, you're too late. You have been the bane of my existence. Being in this marriage for the rest of my life is no different from being tortured by aliens."
Getting more and more desperate Adam tried again. "What about your mother? Are you going to leave her just like that?" he asked frantically.

"All that my mother ever wanted for me was to be happy. I am leaving her a note that will explain everything. I know she will understand."
"Sarah please don't leave me! I'm begging you with all my heart," he said blubbering like a child.

"No," Sarah responded with steel cold eyes.

"What happened to you? How can you be so cruel? I have never seen you like this," he desperately asked.

"What James said, really got to me and that island changed me. It made me strong and the new me has come alive. I just can't take this anymore. I listened to myself on that answering machine. I am so happy. I haven't been happy for a long time, and if there is a way to have that again I am taking that chance." Feeling his heart getting crushed on the inside Adam remained silent. "Is this the kind of life you want for yourself? Cheating on me? Not being able to touch me?" she asked painfully.

"I hate it!" Adam said vehemently, banging on the table. "I hate myself for hurting you."

"Then do something about it, come with me." Sarah replied unable to hide her impatience.

"I can't. Sarah, I have tried so many times and I failed. I watch you sleeping. I push myself to touch you with all my might, but something stops me every time. I see a woman walking by and I try to fight the urge not to want her with everything in me, but I fail all the time," he said sadly.

She walked back to the kitchen table, sat across from her husband, and reached out for both of his hands. "If you come with me to the island you won't fail," she said fervently.

"What if I fail again and I wind up hurting you again?" he asked with desperation in his eyes.

"At least you would have tried Adam, that's what matters," she encouraged him.

"No, I won't do that to myself, I don't have the strength to fight anymore Sarah!" he said, his entire body shaking.

"Well, I still have the strength to fight for what I want. I still believe in us. I believe in the life we have always wanted; in the life we could still have."
Sarah stood up and walked towards her husband, she knelt down and gently held his face. "Lean on me Adam, I am strong enough to believe for the both of us, until you can," she said with conviction.

"It's too late for me." He answered abruptly as he pushed her hands away from his face. Disappointed more that she could express, Sarah gave in, she had done all that she could do. She got up from the floor and went back to her seat.

She looked at Adam through pained eyes and said, "I know it hasn't been easy for you, life has taken so much from you. It's taken your pride, your confidence, and your dreams. It stripped hope and faith out of you, left you jaded and now it's taking your wife *away* from you." Adam could feel the loss of his wife in every fibre of his body. He dropped his head down completely shattered. When he finally had the strength to look up, Sarah was no longer in the kitchen. He was left alone with nothing but regret, darkness, and a deep sadness he had never known.

The Betrayal of a Promise

James wanted nothing more than to enter his father's house, hug him and tell him goodbye. But he knew the only thing they would end up doing was argue. Dad would probably think I've lost my mind and the last thing I want to do is fight with him on our last night together. That's the last memory I want to have. The best thing to do is leave him a note, he said to himself, while backing away from his father's house.

He remembered the appointment he had with Melanie at eight that night. James decided to walk to her place. A storm was coming. James knew from the smell of the air. The trees looked as if they were having a fierce argument, the wind swaying them left and right rapidly. The trees acting out like actors on a stage the fight he was going to have with Melanie, he thought to himself. He buttoned up his jacket and started to run, as the rain began to drizzle. He reached Melanie's house as it was starting to get dark. James knocked at her door.

"Who is it?" Melanie asked in an irritated voice.

"It's me," James answered. Melanie opened her door in a rage.

"How can you do that to me? How can you leave the country without saying a word to me? I have to hear it from your dad that you have gone to some island! What are you thinking!? Did you forget you have responsibilities? Running around like a little boy acting a fool." She carried on shouting at him. James remained silent waiting for her to cool down. "Answer me!" she yelled.

"Are you done?" James quietly asked.

"Yes," Melanie answered disarmed.

"You have every right to be upset with me, but that does not give you the right to disrespect me," he said trying to control his temper from getting the better of him but completely failing. His anger was boiling in the pit of his stomach. "I have had it up to here with you!" James shouted out loud as he lifted his hand towards his neck. "I've' had to deal with you and Dad always wringing my neck. Well not anymore, I am done. Don't ever speak to me that way again," he said sternly looking her straight in the eye.
"I am sorry James," Melanie replied, feeling a little afraid. James had never raised his voice to her before. It was the first time he ever stood up for himself. She actually respected him for the first time. "I was upset when you left. I am sorry, I meant no disrespect," she said, while looking down at the muddy ground.

"It's alright just don't do it again," he replied feeling calmer. "But I am not sorry for leaving town." Melanie was surprised by that response and stared at him in disbelief. The rain was pouring down harder and both of them were drenched from head to toe. "What I am sorry for, is not telling you," he said.

"Can we go inside James? I am wet, cold, and pregnant," she answered irritated and turned to enter her house.

"I am leaving you Melanie," he said.

"You what?" she asked as she turned back to face James. She thought she would give birth at that moment out of shock. Speechless she stared hard at James.

"I am leaving town and I am never coming back," he said. The cold seemed not to affect him at all, nor the fact that Melanie looked like she was going to faint at any minute.

"James if this is about our argument, I am sorry I screamed at you. Couples fight all the time," she lovingly replied. In her mind James was over-reacting.

"We are not a couple," he bluntly replied. "We are not in love. We were fooling around, and you fell pregnant," James candidly answered. She was hurt by his callous manner.

"Wow are you blatantly trying to hurt me? How can you be so vicious?" Melanie painfully asked.

"I am sorry. I am not trying to be cruel, just stating facts," he replied. The serious look on his face clearly showed that he was not joking, and that he was actually leaving her! Melanie thought to herself. If James was thinking of leaving her, he had another thing coming! The pain she had just felt was immediately replaced by pure rage.

178

"You want facts!" Melanie screeched frantically. "I am pregnant with your baby!"

Unflustered by her screams James answered back, "You and the baby will be well taken care of. I am leaving a note, stating that my inheritance is yours and everything that's in my bank account. You can go to art school when the kid is older and pursue your dream of being an artist." He said, trying to bring a ray of hope into the situation. Nothing he said or did could console Melanie in this instance.

"You are going to abandon your own flesh and blood?" she asked, angry tears flowing down her eyes.

"Yes," he nonchalantly answered. His eyes never left hers, he never felt one ounce of shame. Melanie could not believe what was happening to her. She felt betrayed in the most horrible way.

"Our baby is innocent, why are you punishing it for our mistakes!" she hysterically cried out, distraught. Both of them, it seemed, were not bothered by the rain pouring down their faces now. This moment was too intense and important for that to matter. As far as they were concerned, it might as well have been a clear and warm night. James could not help but feel a tinge of pain from her remark.

"I am trying to save this child from myself. What kind of father do you think I will make if I am bitter and angry all the time?" he asked in an emotional tone. "Look at Dad and me, I can't do that to my child. This is my way of doing the right thing," he said in his defence.

Melanie clutching on to her stomach, her face dripping in tears cried out. "This child will hate you for leaving it!"

James shrugged his shoulders and answered. "It will hate me if I stay also." He could not help but be emotional as he said with conviction, "I am going because I want to fulfil my dreams."

"I knew this was all about your own selfish reasons!" she screamed through her tears. "What you want! What you need! News flash, James, life is not about you all the time! You disgust me," she said bitter, heartbroken, and feeling unwanted.

"I am trying to be a good father; the best way I know how. I am trying to protect our child from my resentment, and I will resent it *and* you if I stay. You know the kid will sense that. What do you think that will do to him? This way I am teaching my child to follow his dreams," he defensively replied.

"Oh, spare me your mumbo jumbo James. That's what all deadbeat dads say," she answered arrogantly. "You are abandoning your unborn child, plain and simple! You are as hateful and selfish as your father," she continued, with nothing but disgust for James.

It was hard to hear and even harder to take, James flinched. He realised Melanie knew exactly how to hit hard below the belt. He had never wanted to be anything like his father and Melanie knew that. Silence passed through them like a bird flying between two oak trees. James now stared into her eyes without flinching. At that moment he wanted nothing more than to hurt her as badly as she hurt him. If she was not pregnant, I would be beating the hell out of her at this moment, he contemplated. James realised she was speaking out of pain, and he could understand that at the end of the day he was making her raise his child alone. Who wouldn't be angry at that? The least he could do was to be compassionate, he reflected. He could feel himself being at ease again.

"I am sorry you feel that way," he quietly replied.

"Huh," she mocked.

He understood how she was feeling, and it was easy to forgive her for being cruel. "I hope one day you will find it in your heart to forgive me," he said sincerely.
"If you leave now, I will never forgive you for as long as I live, I swear it, James!" she answered.

James gave a slight nod and calmly said, "Goodbye Melanie." He turned his back and walked away.

"James don't leave! James please don't go! You promised to marry me! James!" she hysterically and frantically called out into the night, as she watched him walking away from her. Begging and pleading she screamed out "Think of your child!"

His reply was only heard by the rain falling on his face as he took another step away from Melanie. "I am," James whispered.

Chapter 5

The Night Before

The night she had always dreamed of was finally here, the night all her dreams would come true, the night she would give herself to the man she loved, her husband. But she didn't love Derrick and he was not her husband, yet. Now the beautiful dream had turned into a horrible nightmare, she quietly reflected as she fixed her hair in the mirror. She chose to wear a black short dress. Black seemed appropriate for the evening. She might as well be going to a funeral since her dreams were all dying tonight, she said to herself. The phone startled her from her morbid thinking.

Jessica answered the phone. "Hello."

"Hey babe, ready for our big night?" It was Derrick, and his excitement could not be hidden from his voice.

"I am just getting ready. I am on my way," she replied shyly.

"Change of plans," Derrick replied. "I am outside your door."

"You came here in the pouring rain?" she asked in complete surprise.

"What's a little rain? I just could not wait to see you. Come over here and let me in," he seductively replied.

"OK," she said and dropped the phone, her heart was beating so fast as she walked steadily to the front door and tried to keep her hands from shaking as she opened the door.

Derrick stepped into the house with a huge smile on his face and took off his wet jacket. "It's warm in here, and you look scorching hot," he said as he gently took her hand and placed a kiss of anticipation on its palm. Jessica felt her blood running cold the minute his lips touched her hand. "There is nothing to be afraid of," he whispered, like the devil incarnate luring his victim into a trap. "So how about we go to the bedroom?" Derrick said, acting all suave.

"I could cook, we could have dinner first," she said as she tried to pull her hand away, but he held on tightly.

"No there is no need for that. We have dined all over town. Tonight, is about us, our night, and it will make our wedding day even more special."

"OK," she sadly agreed with a nod. "Can I offer you something to drink?" She tried again to pull her hand from his grip, but Derrick grabbed her by the waist and pulled her towards himself and crushingly held on to her waist. "You're stalling," he whispered into her ear.

"I am, I guess I am just so scared," she answered as she avoided looking him in the eye.

"What is there to be afraid of?" he asked. "Let's act our age, shall we?" he replied in his patronizing voice. "We don't want to start the evening on a bad note. Do we?" he said in a menacing manner. Jessica timidly shook her head.

"That's my girl," he said with a satisfied smile on his face. Taking her by the hand, Derrick started walking towards the bedroom. Like a lamb led to the slaughter she submissively followed. Her insides were tied like a knot, her stomach feeling ill and legs trembling. Her conversation with James instantly started playing in her head. Never give up on your dreams. Never stop fighting, she heard James say over and over again in her head.

Never give up on your dreams. Never stop fighting,

These words became louder and louder. She felt as if her skull was going to crack. Jessica could not take it any longer. "STOP!" she screamed, silencing the voice in her head just as they entered her room.

"What's' wrong now!" Derrick raised his voice.

Everything James said to her in the car felt right. She knew she could not sleep with Derrick when her husband was waiting for her inside that birdhouse, back at the island, she thought to herself.

"I can't do this Derrick," she murmured.

"Oh, don't give me that!" Derrick rudely replied. "We've talked about this, and I have had just about enough! Didn't I say I am going to marry you?" he hollered like a mad man.

She could feel her fear choking the breath out of her, but she mastered all the courage she had inside and said, "This is not me. I thought I could, but I can't." She raised her voice a little higher, her determination pushing her on. "I don't want to be your wife by having to sleep with you. I don't want to be your wife at all," she said frankly. "We are too different, we will make each other unhappy and it's time we end this!"

Derrick could not believe the words coming out of her mouth. It took him a minute to answer. "*Now* you break up with me?! Wow, you have great timing," he replied sarcastically.
"It wasn't planned. I never meant to hurt you," she said sincerely.

"No, you didn't hurt me. You helped me realize what you really are," he answered in a condescending tone. "You have completely deluded yourself," he said laughing. "You need to grow up, and fast Jessica."

"This has nothing to do with age. It's a choice, my choice," she replied passionately.

"You are such a tease Jessica. You think I spent my money and my time so that you can change your mind?" he screamed as he seized her and pinned both her arms to her back.

"You're hurting me!" she cried out while struggling to pull away from him.

"Women like you need to be taught a lesson. You have been brain-washed by that ridiculous religion of yours, and it stops now."

Derrick picked her up and walked towards the bed. "What are you doing? Let go of me," she yelled kicking and screaming. He reached the bed and brutally threw her on the bed.

"Don't... Derrick, I am begging you!" she cried out helplessly, tears pouring down her face.

"You will thank me later," he said as he climbed on top of her and held down her hands. She lay there thinking, it's over, Derrick is stronger than me. It felt as if she had been thrown inside a deep dark hole and there was no one to rescue her. There would be no escape from this. Derrick started to unbutton his shirt and with each button she felt he was ripping away at her heart and dreams. Her dream was dying right in front of her and there was nothing she could do. The realization of what was happening to her broke her to pieces. The feeling of despair cutting into her soul.

Her conversation with James vividly and suddenly played into her mind again. This time she didn't just hear him, but she could see him in the car telling her to fight. He was saying "Fight till the end for your dream."

Derrick started to kiss her forcefully all over her face and neck. The memory playing in her mind urged her to fight with all she had. She bit Derrick hard on the ear! He screeched like a wounded dog. He could not take the pain and climbed off her, but she vengefully held on to his ear and a piece of his ear was torn off in the process.

"AAH!" he screamed in agony. Derrick fell to his knees holding his bleeding ear squirming on the floor.
Jessica jumped off the bed. She was desperate. She needed to make sure he stayed on the floor. He would get up any second and attack her again, she realised. Jessica ran to the dressing table and without any hesitation picked up the chair. It was very heavy, and her arms began to hurt. All she needed to do was hold it long enough to reach Derrick, she thought as she walked towards him. She managed to reach him, but he was not looking at her.
"Derrick!" she yelled. Derrick turned and faced her with his vindictive eyes full of rage , Jessica dropped the chair on him, and he collapsed on his stomach. The chair had fallen on his head and rendered him unconscious. Jessica grabbed her car
keys from her bedside table and ran out of the house like a forest catching on fire. She didn't dare look back. The pouring rain and thunderstorm did not hinder her from sprinting to her car. By the time she reached her vehicle she was dripping wet. She decided to drive to the house of the only man she trusted in the world, the man who fought for her and her dreams, the man who was more than a friend, a brother. She was going to James.

Finding Refuge

James thought a change of scenery might help him with the trouble he was having, which was writing the last letter he would ever write to his dad. He thought if he left his room and sat in the lounge, the words would automatically appear on the blank page staring back at him. He kept tapping his pen on the table, aggravated that the only word he managed to scribble on the top of the page was "Dad". The rest of the words refused to manifest, no matter how hard he tried.

"He is my dad at the end of the day, as difficult as he is, and to say goodbye to him...." he said thinking out loud. James didn't finish what he was about to say because he heard a knock at the door. "Who could it be at this time of the night," he wondered as he walked to the door. "Who is it?"

"It's me, James," Jessica answered.

"What!" he said and quickly opened the door. He was startled to find Jessica wet and shivering at his doorstep.

"What are you doing here?" he asked.

"Can I come in?" Jessica answered, her whole body shaking.

"I am sorry; I'm just so surprised to see you here. Come in," he hastily replied. Jessica quickly stepped inside the house. "You're soaking wet," he remarked with a worried look in his face. "You need to get out of that dress. Let's go to my room and you can change into some warm pants and shirt. We have to be quiet my dad is sleeping," he whispered as he walked to his room with Jessica not too far behind him. They entered his room, and James laid out a pair of his pants and shirt on the bed. "I'll give you some privacy," he said walking towards the door.

"Wait, can I use your cell phone? It's really important, something happened to me tonight."

"Of course!" he replied and gave her the phone.

"Thanks," she replied appreciatively as she took it.

"You're welcome." He walked out of the room and closed the door behind him.

Jessica called the police anonymously. "Hello, I heard screaming coming out of my neighbours' house. The address is 147 Church Street, Houghton Avenue. Please hurry it sounds as if a woman is being attacked," she said and quickly dropped the phone before the police could trace the call. The police would go to her house and take Derrick to the hospital. She could not leave him there to die, even if he tried to rape her. It was the right thing to do, she thought to herself as she changed into the warm clothes James laid out for her.

In a few minutes there was a knock at the door. She opened it and found James holding two cups; coffee and hot cocoa. He gave her one cup. She took a sip and tasted the hot cocoa. "Thank you, James, I love hot cocoa. I truly needed this especially tonight," she said appreciatively while sitting on the bed. James sat next to her.

"So, what happened?" he asked.

"Derrick tried to rape me," she replied.

"What!" James yelled out.

"I told him I couldn't go through with it anymore, and he became violent."

"He did what! I am going to kill him."

"Don't bother, he is lying unconscious in my house."

"What!"

"I hit him with a chair, and he fell unconscious. I just called the police to my house, they will call an ambulance to take him to the hospital in case he is badly hurt," she said nervously.

"He got exactly what he deserved," James replied adamantly.

"I can't go back home after what happened. I am frazzled. The police will want answers and I just can't handle that right now," she said as she wiped a tear from her eye.

"You're staying here tonight," he replied in his protective tone. "Can I ask you something?" he asked lovingly.

"Sure," she answered.

"What made you change your mind?" he asked curiously.

"You," she said with a smile, her spirits lifting up. "What you said to me made sense and I knew I couldn't go through with it anymore."

"Did he hurt you?"
"No. There were moments I thought that it was all over, but your voice pushed me to keep fighting. I fought for my dream because of you," she said tearfully.
"Come here," he lovingly replied as he gave her a hug. He added sincerely, "I am sorry I wasn't there to help you."

"You were there, every second," she said as she looked into his eyes. She teared up again. "I can't thank you enough," she said, and gave him an affectionate embrace.
"That's what brothers are for," he lovingly replied, brushing the back of her head.

Jessica sat up straight and said, "I'm coming with you tomorrow."

"To the island?" he asked in excitement.

"Yes," she said with a giggle.
"Oh Jessica, I am so proud of you," he said and hugged her again.

"Thank you, I am proud of me too, it's been quite a day," she said with a tired yawn.

"You have been through a lot tonight, you must be worn out some, and besides, we have a big day tomorrow. I'll take the couch."

"OK,'' she said as she climbed into the bed. As soon as she closed her eyes she fell into a deep sleep. James tiptoed out of his room, making sure he didn't wake her up. He was determined to finish his letter and walked decisively back to the lounge. James was inspired by the courage Jessica had exhibited that day, and he found the strength to write what he had wanted to say to his father for years. He wrote from the heart.

Dad
I know losing mom left a hole in your heart that nobody could fill, and that's why you pushed me away. I don't hate you. You did the best you could do, but I can't allow life to do to me what it did to you. When you wake up, I will be gone, and I am never coming back. I will always love you and I am asking you to be the father you could not be with me, to my child. All I have belongs to the baby, including the inheritance you leave me in the future. Mom wouldn't want us to be bitter. This is my way of honouring her memory. I am my mother's son, and I am doing what she taught me, to be true to myself. I hope you find the strength to honour her the right way and that's being happy Dad.
Your son
James.

Going Home

James slowly walked to his father's room and quietly opened the door. He placed the letter on top of the pillow that was once his mother's side of the bed and watched his father sleeping for an hour, memorising every single facet of his
fathers' face. When he felt pacified, he rose, moved closer to kiss the old man's forehead, thought twice about it lest he wake him, and strode confidently out of the room and out of his father's life.

Chapter 5

Chapter **6**

Parting Ways

Right on the dot, the alarm on the bedside table started ringing at five thirty. Sarah woke up with a smile on her face for the very first time and she reached out and turned it off. She could not help humming a happy tune as she took a quick shower. The promise of today made her tingle all over with exhilaration as she slipped into a pair of jeans and her favourite jersey. It only hit her, as she reached the kitchen to make a cup of coffee, that her husband was nowhere in sight. She could feel her heart breaking as she stood in the very same kitchen, she had seen Adam fall apart. He left without saying goodbye, she sadly thought to herself. Sarah walked around the house she had called home for a very long time. Each room she entered held a painful memory. She wanted to leave everything behind her and did not even pack one item of clothing. The only thing she wanted to take with her was her husband, but he had given up on their marriage. It was time to let go of her past and start anew, she reflected.

Her heart skipped a beat as soon as she saw the limo park in her driveway at six thirty. Sarah ran out of her house without even looking back. The door was opened as she entered the car and to her surprise someone else was inside. She thought it was James, but she had the shock of her life when the stranger turned around to face her and she realised it was Adam!

"What are you doing here?" she screamed with delight.

"It turns out I still have some fight left in me," he said with tears in his eyes. Her heart was filled with such joy she thought it would burst. She leapt into his arms and was surprised when he responded to her embrace and held her even tighter.

"I never loved you more than I do in this moment Adam," she said as the tears fell on their accord down her cheeks.

"The thought of never seeing you again just killed me," he said tearfully.

"I can face anything with you by my side Sarah. Even aliens!" he said as he laughed. "But to live without you, that I can never do," he said passionately.

"It's not aliens," she said with a giggle.

"We'll see," Adam said with a nervous laugh.

"We shall, you and me," she smiled as she confidently held tightly to his hand. The limo driver stepped out and closed their door. Both of them were scared and excited, as the limo started to drive to the airport.

Sarah and Adam walked hand in hand, expecting to find one passenger in the plane which was James. They were astounded to find Jessica sitting with James sipping champagne. She stood up from her seat with a wide grin on her face and raised her champagne glass as she said, "Surprise!"

"You came!" Sarah said out loud as she ran to Jessica. James moved out of the way with his champagne glass, as the two women collided in a loving embrace. Jessica spilled some of the champagne on Sarah, but they were both too happy to care.

"So did you!" Jessica exclaimed. The air hostess smiled at Adam and handed him two glasses of champagne. He cautiously walked towards Sarah and handed her a glass.

"Adam, I am so glad you came," Jessica said and gave him an affectionate hug.

"I can't believe it myself, but here I am," Adam replied. "What changed your mind?" he asked.

"James," she said still wearing a grin on her face. The two men looked at each other and laughed out loud.

"Well, I didn't expect to see you here. I guess you are not afraid of aliens anymore," James remarked in a teasing tone.

"I guess I deserve that," Adam said as he smiled. His playful smile was replaced by a serious expression. "James, listen I'd like to apologize for everything."

"Hey man there is no need for that. I was way out of line anyway." James quickly responded.

"No, you were right. I am just glad you had the guts to say it," Adam said as he gestured towards Sarah to come stand next to him. Adam held on to her waist as soon as Sarah stood next to him. "I thank you for giving my wife her voice and for giving me the whipping I deserved," he said, and everybody burst out laughing including Adam. "Thank you, James, from the bottom of my heart. It wasn't easy to hear, but you opened my eyes."

"You're the reason we are both here," Sarah said lovingly as happy tears fell down her checks combined with laughter.

"Aah, it was nothing," James replied trying to make light of the whole conversation.

"You're the reason we are all here," Jessica exclaimed. "Everybody raise your glasses I want to make a toast," she said. Everyone raised their glasses at the same time. "To James, you are the reason all of us have something we thought we had lost. You gave our hope back to us. You have the heart of a lion, wise beyond your years, a man of sheer determination, and conviction," she said sincerely.

"Don't forget stubborn," Adam jokingly remarked and everyone laughed.

"*Very* stubborn," Jessica said with a smile. "Thank you for making us believe that our lives can change for the better," she continued. "You never once gave up on what we all experienced on that island. We were all against you, fighting you at every turn. You were the voice we refused to listen to, and we treated you like the enemy," she said emotionally. "Yet you turned out to be our unlikely hero. The messenger of God, telling us never to give up no matter how dark it gets." Her voice started breaking. "Wherever this journey may take us I want you to know, that I love you and I will never forget you. I am so proud to call you, my brother." Tears started to fall down Jessica's face like stars falling from the sky as she passionately exclaimed, "To James, our unlikely hero!" Adam and Sarah's eyes swirled up with tears too, as they cried out at the same time, "To James our unlikely hero!"

"You got to respond to that toast man," Adam said as he wiped a tear from his eye. "Jessica, look at what you have done. You've made a grown man cry."

"Oh yes, please James," Sarah lovingly remarked, sitting next to her husband.

"I absolutely agree," Jessica replied with a silly grin on her face as she sat down.

James was the only one left standing as he started with his speech.

"Wow, after that, I don't know what to say," he responded emotionally holding back his tears. "First, I must say it's good to have the gang back together again. We started this journey together and we are ending it together. That's the way it should be," he said with certainty. "No matter what may be waiting for us on that island. We have won because we are all here and I believe whatever is out there, is worth fighting for," James continued as he pointed outside the window, "worth believing in. Our fears almost kept us from going, but we are all here, not one of us is left behind," he said throatily as he lovingly looked at their faces. "So, let's go out there and take what's ours!" he said passionately. "Let's live the life we want and deserve! We could be facing death out there but our dreams are worth that risk." He said valiantly. He wept as he looked at the three faces looking back at him with pride, conviction, and love. He raised his glass high up and announced like a war hero: "To the island and everything it brings!"

Tears in their eyes, Jessica, Adam, and Sarah stood up, raised their glasses, and cried out: "To the island and everything it brings!" This brought out another burst of laughter and extreme joy as they all left their seats and embraced James.

Their screams of joy and laughter could be heard as far as the cockpit. They started hugging each other with tears spilling down their faces. They huddled up together as a group and shouted out simultaneously: "To the island!"

"Ladies and gentlemen, please fasten your seat belts as the plane is preparing for lift off," they heard the voice of the air hostess over the intercom interrupting their camaraderie. Everybody excitedly hurried back to their seats and the plane gracefully soared into the sky with four very special people. The conversation on the plane lasted throughout the night. Everybody knew they would never see each other again and made each moment count. The sun came up and greeted the blue sky. They heard the pilot saying the words they had been waiting to hear through the intercom, "Ladies and gentlemen we have nearly reached our destination and we are now preparing for landing. The plane miraculously landed on the beach without a runway.

Sarah looked outside the window and called out, "We are on the island!"

"That's impossible," James replied as he leaned over Jessica, to take a better look. "She's' right, we are on the beach!"

"How can a plane land in the middle of a beach?" Adam asked in sheer amazement.

"Is there anything realistic about any of our experiences, since we won that competition," Jessica replied in amazement as she looked at all of them.

"Isn't that the truth," Sarah agreed as she looked at Jessica.

Jessica continued to speak," I mean we won a cruise for eating a specific brand of chocolate. Who wins a trip for eating a brand of chocolate? It was just a way of getting us here!" Jessica said in wonder.

Sarah was utterly amazed by everything that happened to them. "Whatever is responsible for bringing us here succeeded," Adam said with foreboding and wondering what was waiting for them under the ocean.

"God did this, guys," Jessica answered with assuredness. A short silence followed, no one said anything. "Anyway, that's what I believe," she remarked unapologetically.

"You could be right," James replied as she looked at her.

"Let's not jump to conclusions now," Adam said, being the voice of doom as he stared at everyone in fear. "Little green men could still be waiting for us in that water. Waiting to torture us," he continued as he pointed to the ocean.

"Or it could be something beautiful," Sarah responded to her husband's fears. She continued her eyes full of hope, "Jessica is right. All of us felt compelled to buy a piece of chocolate because it was called *Destiny* and the name of the ship is *Believe*. Does that sound like something foreboding to you, or something wonderful and Holy?"

"I really want to believe you Sarah, but the truth is we just don't know," Adam replied emotionally as he tightly held onto her hand.

James gallantly stood up and said, "None of us are going to get answers by sitting here. Let's go and meet our destiny." James did not wait another minute longer. He walked out of the plane, with the others not too far behind him. Their feet landed on the soft sandy beach. The sun felt like it had a smile on its face when they looked at the incredible beauty surrounding them. The tropical palm trees looked like the hands of God calling them home. The gigantic mountains surrounding the island and the indigenous tropical flowers and plants took their breath away. It was as if they were seeing the island the way a new-born child sees the world for the very first time. They could see the "BELIEVE" super yacht in the middle of the ocean from where they were standing. James looked across the water silently. His eyes fixed on the ship, deep in thought. Jessica was standing next to him.

"A penny for your thoughts?" she said and nudged him on the arm with her shoulder.

James put his hands in his pocket and his face started forming a smile as he said, "I am certain that the exact spot of the birdhouse is under the ship. All we have to do is swim straight towards the *Believe*.

The four friends looked out into the deep blue sea, each remembering their experience under the ocean. Without any warning at all James started running straight for the water, yelling and screaming in sheer delight, taking off his shoes in the process. The rest followed suit, jubilation and hope filling their senses as they threw their shoes in the air. They laughed out loud as they ran to James who was standing at the edge of the water, waiting for them. Adam and Sarah hugged James at the same time. "Take care of each other," James said as he hugged them back in return. Adam and Sarah nodded simultaneously, their faces saying everything they could not say. Jessica watched the emotional scene unfolding before her eyes and her tears started gushing down her face.

James turned to Jessica and cupped her face as he wiped her tears with his other hand. "I will never forget you too," he said as he placed her closely to his chest and held her tightly.

"You changed my life James," Jessica cried out bitterly.

"That's what brothers are for, big sis," he answered as his voice broke.

"I am going to miss hearing those words," she said as her tears fell like a waterfall down her face. Jessica covered her face in his shirt hoping it would muffle her crying, to no avail. James gently rocked her softly as he allowed his tears to make their own entrance on his face. There was no dry eye in sight. Even Adam couldn't hold back his tears watching brother and sister saying goodbye.

Letting go was the hardest thing to do for the both of them but they finally let go of each other. "Enough with the tears, this is supposed to be a happy occasion." James said while laughing through his tears.

"You're right," Jessica replied trying to keep the tears at bay. She walked to Sarah and threw her hands around her neck. "Goodbye Sarah, you deserve all the love and happiness you are going to get," Jessica said through her tears.

"Oh Jessica, I am going to miss you so much. You have become my best friend and I wish you a love as beautiful as your heart," Sarah cried out. The long embrace ended, and Jessica lovingly looked at Adam.

"Mr Sceptical," she said with a smile as she opened her arms and hugged him. Adam laughed in response and held on to her even tighter. "I pray for a faith that destroys all that doubt in your heart," Jessica said as another tear fell down her cheek.

"Me too," he emotionally replied.
"Goodbye," she said and walked back to James.
Without saying another word, the four friends held each other's hands and walked to the ocean. They swam towards the ship. When they could not feel the sand beneath their feet an overpowering force immediately pulled them deep under the water. The invisible entity pulled them to the bottom of the ocean and a new feeling greeted their souls. It was peace. The wooden birdhouse was still lying on the ground, as if it were lying there all along waiting for them. It was still a thrill to walk under water as they all huddled together.

James was the first to break from their embrace and shook Adam's hand and hugged Sarah one last time. As much as they all wanted to say their last goodbyes, they couldn't talk under water. James pulled Jessica close to his chest for the very last time, looking up he gave her a smile she'd remember all her life. A smile full of love and admiration. Jessica smiled back as wildly as she could, to express all the love she was feeling. She knew fully well, that at that moment

James was taking a picture with his eyes. A picture he would store in his mind that would last for a lifetime. Slowly breaking away from Jessica, he started walking towards the birdhouse and picked it up.

Turning to the three people he cared for deeply, James raised his hand and waved goodbye. They all waved back at the same time. The love they all had for one other was written in their faces. All of them, thinking the same thing at the same time. This will be the last time they would ever be together again. With a broken heart James turned his full attention to the birdhouse. The window started drawing him closer and closer inside the house, pulling him into itself. The three of them watched as James' entire body disappeared into the birdhouse. With that the birdhouse slowly floated to the ground.

Jessica motioned for Sarah and Adam to pick up the small wooden object. The couple embraced her one more time and hand in hand Adam and Sarah walked to the house. She picked it up with one hand and held on to her husband's hand with the other. They both looked at the window and Sarah wanted to see if Adam was having second thoughts and gave him a quick glance. She was glad to find his eyes totally engrossed in the tiny window. Jessica watched as the couple were pulled inside the window at the same time and disappeared. The birdhouse slowly floated down to the ground.

In awe Jessica watched the birdhouse roll closer and closer towards her feet until it touched her toes. It was calling to her, telling her it was her turn, she said thinking to herself. She looked around the empty ocean and realized her only companions were the fish swimming around her. All of her friends were gone, she was left alone. She slowly and fearfully picked it up and looked into the window. Jessica brought it closer and closer to her face. A sensation of extreme joy filled her heart as the house pulled her deeper and deeper in. This time there was no fear or resistance as the house pulled her inside. The same vision appearing before her eyes was as clear as day. She saw herself wearing a wedding ring on her left finger. Her husband and her fully clothed, reading the bible sitting on their bed. There were no thoughts of turning back or pulling away entering her mind this time, only the deep desire and need to be part of that beautiful picture filled her heart. Her desire and want became stronger and stronger as the house drew her entire body through the little window. A white blinding light filled the house as her feet disappeared into the window. The birdhouse floated down to the ground. Everything was quiet, the fish peacefully swimming along as if nothing miraculous had just happened.

Chapter **7**

The Other World

*J*essica could not help but wake up, her baby was kicking her inside her pregnant belly. "Is it time for milk and cookies sweetheart?" she said as she lovingly touched her stomach. She started talking to her baby the day she found out that she was pregnant. Nothing could measure the love she had for her unborn baby. She usually had cravings for milk and cookies exactly around six o'clock in the morning. Her baby would start kicking and she knew exactly what it wanted. Jessica slowly slipped off the bed, trying not to wake her loving husband Joshua who was sleeping beside her. She walked to the kitchen and found a glass of milk and a plate of cookies on the table waiting for her. Joshua was so attentive he would wake up before her and place the cookies and milk on the table then go back to bed. She was just about to remove the saucer on top of her glass when a familiar powerful sensation drew her to her lounge. As she walked to the lounge she reflected over her life. She could not believe that her life of misery had turned to joy. She was living in bliss, feeling like the most blessed woman in the world. The tears she used to cry could fill an ocean, but she didn't mind the tears falling down her face, like petals falling on a beautiful garden, because joy always accompanied these tears. Jessica entered the lounge and looked at her wedding pictures hanging all over the walls.

Jessica recognised the overwhelming peaceful sensation. It was the same powerful force she felt from the birdhouse. The sensational force pushed her towards the TV set. The TV screen turned on by itself. The pictures on the screen were divided into three sections. Tears of joy filled her eyes as she recognised the faces appearing on her screen. On the left side of the TV screen, she saw James singing on a stage. Overwhelmed by what she was seeing, she sat down. James was in a concert, looking like a rock star! He wore black shiny jeans and a white studded t-shirt. He was singing his heart out to a multitude of people, dancing and singing along with him. His face was full of passion as he sang the song, "Is it love" by Whitesnake. Jessica's laughter filled the room like clouds drifting in the sky. She started singing along with James. *"Is it love that I am feeling? Is this the love that I've been searching for? Is this love or am I dreaming? This must be love because it's really got a hold on me. A hold on me."* It was amazing! The crowd shouted and applauded as he bowed down after he finished singing. James took everything in as he looked at the appreciative crowd. His face exuberated nothing but sheer contentment. Jessica knew James was living his slice of heaven wherever he was.

Her right screen showed a couple fawning all over each other. It was Adam and Sarah jogging in the park. A couple of young beautiful woman ran past them, but Adam only had eyes for one woman, his wife. Jessica could see all the love Adam had for Sarah in his eyes. Sarah responded with laughter like bubbles coming from a champagne glass as Adam covered her with kisses and hugs. The bottom screen showed Jessica's wedding day from beginning to the end.

"I Jessica Washington, take you Joshua Stevens to be my lawfully wedded husband," she saw herself saying her vows. She remembered every moment of that day; tears of joy invaded her face once again.

Suddenly the screens changed. She saw James looking so handsome in white pants and shirt covered in black diamonds. Adam and Sarah had their exercise gear. Each of them was on a different side of the screens. On the left James was looking at his TV screen at his mansion and on the right Adam and Sarah were watching the TV from their house.

"I don't believe what I am seeing! James, can you hear me?" she cried out in delight.
"Yes, I can," he said with a big smile on his face.

"We can too," Sarah said as she waved at them.

"The gang is back together again. We all made it guys!" James screamed.

"Jessica you are married! I saw your wedding on the screen," Sarah exclaimed.

"And five months pregnant," she said as she stood up, making sure everybody could see her pregnant belly.

"I am so happy for you," Sarah said in sheer amazement.

"Clearly you two are happily in love. You can't keep your hands off each other," Jessica said, happy for her friend.

"Looks like you are on your second honeymoon," James said in his teasing tone.

"I am a man in love and a faithful one," Adam proudly replied.

"And a pastor as well," Sarah happily added
.

"What!" Jessica and James yelled out at the same time; they were both thoroughly shocked.

"It's true. My wonderful husband accepted Jesus as his Lord and Saviour. We have never been so happy and so in love!" she continued, her smile never leaving her face.

"What about you? Mr. Rock Star," Adam said. It was his turn now to tease James.

"James, you sang our song," Jessica emotionally remarked. "You were fantastic! I know your mother is so proud of you in heaven," Jessica said as fresh tears appeared in her face.

"We did it sis! We found the love we have been searching for! You were the most beautiful bride I've ever seen on your wedding day. I wished I were there, "James said, as his voice broke with happy tears in his eyes.

"Thank you. I wanted you there myself, all of you. But no one remembers you in Hopetown. It's like you never existed," Jessica sadly answered.

"That's impossible! You are in Hopetown! I live in Hopetown!" James said in shock.

"We live in Hopetown too, but no one knows James or you Jessica here," Sarah said in amazement.

"This means we all live in different versions of the same exact town," Adam replied astounded.

"That explains things," James said. "In my version Dad is supportive of my music. We get along and Melanie is not pregnant. She is a famous painter who visits the town now and then. She does not even recognise me," James continued.

"Same here. Derrick does not know me and is married to someone else," Jessica answered.

"No one remembers I was the playboy of the century here," Adam said.

"The only imperfect thing about this world is that you guys are not here," Jessica said as she sighed. Everyone's face showed the sadness they were feeling. At that moment Jessica had an epiphany and her mood brightened up like a light bulb. "I need to tell you something," she said in excitement. "I prayed to God to save me from my miserable life before I won the competition. I have the feeling I was not the only one," she said as she looked at everyone.

"My mother and I prayed for God's help in my kitchen before we won," Sarah said in awe.

"I did too. I didn't believe he existed, but I prayed anyway," Adam added.

"James, that leaves only you?" Jessica asked.

"I certainly did," James said proudly.

"I don't' believe this. We all said the same prayer," Jessica said in sheer amazement.

"I guess we all agree God is the reason we are here and not aliens!" Adam said with conviction.

"I am proud to say I agree with my husband," Sarah cheerfully responded.

"I say a big Yes and Amen to that!" James replied in excitement.

"I know so many people who need this kind of miracle. I have one particular family in mind. The Andersons. They have a very sick boy, his name is David He was a student of mine. We used to have private lessons through digital communication because of his illness." Jessica said in a serious tone.

"I heard about the Anderson boy. He can't be around too many people or even leave his home. It has something to do with the bacteria in the atmosphere. He could die if he left his house. You are right Jessica. This is bigger than us guys." James replied.

"Oh this just breaks my heart. The poor boy. The has to be something we can do?" Sarah asked

"We all prayed and asked God for help. We should all pray for the Anderson family. God can use the birdhouse to help David too and so many others" Adam replied

"I agree we should all make pact starting today to pray for the Anderson family and everyone who finds themselves in the same situation we were in."

They all nodded their heads in agreement.

"I thought God had forgotten about me," Jessica said as new tears exploded on her face. "It turns out He remembered us all! He never gave up on us or our dreams, even when we thought there was no hope. He had a plan and purpose for all of us," she said passionately.

"It reminds me of the scripture in the bible," Adam responded. He started saying the scripture from his memory. "Jeremiah 29 verse 11. I alone know the plans I have for you, plans to bring you prosperity and not disaster, plans to bring about the future you hope for."

Everybody could not help the tears of joy falling down their faces. God had touched their lives in such a miraculous way. He had given them a second chance in life. "I think we should all close our eyes and say a personal prayer. Thanking Him for what he has done for all of us," Adam humbly said. Everybody bowed their heads and silently prayed.

When everybody stopped praying James said, "I have a feeling this is going to be the last time we are going to see each other." Everybody nodded in agreement. "I hate goodbyes. So, all I am going to say is, be happy and I love all of you," he said covering his pain with a smile.

"I can't think of anything better to say. So, to all of you I love you and be happy. Thanks, bro for everything," Jessica replied. Her love and sadness were written all over her face, like a poem being read out loud.

Sarah whispered something to Adam and both of them said at the same time, "Be happy James and Jessica, we will always love you!" Everyone started laughing through the tears, blowing kisses to each other as their TV screens turned off on their own.

Adam and Sarah left the house and went for their morning jog, kissing passionately in the park as they ran. James walked out of his house and entered his limousine which was waiting to take him to his next concert. Jessica wiped her tears from her face and went back to bed. She knew her favourite part of her morning was just about to happen. Joshua was about to open his eyes. When her husband finally opened his eyes, it was always like the sun glowing in all its brightness greeting the sky.

"Hey you," he longingly said.

Chapter **8**

David's Escape

*B*ad things happen to good people or should I say horrible, excruciating, heart-breaking ordeals happen to good people. It does not matter how devoted you are to God. Pain will find you wherever you are, and it will sink its claws into you and never let you go, Jennifer thought to herself as she watched her eight-year-old son sleeping, as she was sitting at the edge of the bed. David was her beautiful angel. Her miracle, a blessing from God. She prayed to the Lord to have a son and God answered her prayers, but God forgot to mention a few details. That David would have a debilitating disease that made him a hostage of his own bed. Nor did He mention the fact that she would watch her son living in torment, seeing other little boys play outside having fun, while he watched from the window unable to participate. She could feel the anger and bitterness eating her from the inside. Was this a curse? Or was David being punished? What could David have done in his little life to cause God to be so angry, she wondered as her angry tears started to fall down her cheeks. No. David's fate had been decided for him a long time ago, written in God's heart when Jennifer fell to her knees and prayed for a little boy. Destined by God before David had dreams of his own, before she and her loving husband could imagine a life full of friends, seeing him graduate and have a family of his own in the future. God had already decided her son's fate. She allowed these thoughts to run through her mind and weave a web of darkness around her mind. Tasting her salty tears on her lips and afraid she might wake up David, she walked out of his room, trying with every step to regain her composure as she walked back to her bedroom

She found Mark sitting up, leaning his back on the bed post. He was reading The Daily Chronicle on his tablet.

"Hey," he said lovingly, "I could not sleep he stopped abruptly, noticing the drawn look on his wife's face.

"I was in David's room," she said morosely.

"I thought so. How is he?" Mark asked with concern.

"Sound asleep. Throwing up half the night must have really made him tired," she replied.

"But is he OK now?" Mark asked with a worried tone.

"He is," Jennifer replied reassuringly.

Chapter 8

"Come back to bed," he lovingly said as he reached his hand towards her.

"I have to prepare David's medication."

Mark picked up his watch from the bed side table and said, "It's four in the morning. It's too early for that. Besides, I can do it."

"You need to get ready for work."

"It's Saturday. I am not going to the office."

"Oh, I forgot."

"Please come back to bed," Mark lovingly pleaded. Jennifer snuggled into the covers with her husband. She quickly turned her back away from him, trying to hide the fact that she had been crying. "You have been crying," Mark said.

"No, why would you say that?" she lied.

"Then look at me," Mark demanded.
"No," she replied, "I am just tired."

"I don't believe you," he persisted. "I know you too well. I am your husband and I love you. Look at me Jen," he said as he turned her towards him and switched on the bedside lamp. Her cheeks and face were red from crying. "I was right, you have been crying, Oh

Jennifer. Why do you do this to yourself?'' Mark said trying to be brave for his wife.

"I can't help myself. He is our little boy, and he does not deserve this," Jennifer replied while she covered her face with her hands. Her sobs started to become louder.

"Come here," he said softly. Mark took his wife into his robust arms and cradled her like a little baby. Jennifer's small-figured body fitted perfectly into his well-muscled chest. Jennifer allowed all her pain and anguish to flow out of her. "I know sweetheart; it's going to be alright." Seeing his wife in so much torment tore him to pieces, but he had to be strong. He held on tightly to her until Jennifer cried herself to sleep. An hour later he slowly walked to his son's room. "Hey buddy, wake up its time for your medication," Mark said as he placed the milky white liquid in a glass that he had prepared, on top of his son's bedside table. Jennifer was still fast asleep. David hated this time of the morning and Mark knew why.

"No, I hate it," David grumped as he opened his big droopy dark brown eyes.

"I know son, but it's good for you," Mark replied, giving David an encouraging smile.

"It tastes awful," David mumbled as he covered his face under the covers.

"If you drink it in one gulp you can have a piece of chocolate," his father replied.

"That's blackmail," David said as he popped his head up from his blankets.
"Did it work?" his Dad asked with a smile.

"Only if I can eat the whole slab," David replied with a cheeky grin.

"No, your mom will kill me."

"Please Dad," his son pleaded.

"You had a bad night Davie. Let's not push things OK." Mark said as he brushed his son's black hair.

David was the spitting image of his mother. He didn't have his blond hair or his blue eyes but had his mother's enchanting brown eyes and pitch black hair. Except for his pale sickly skin and tiny body, Mark thought to himself.

"Oh, come on, Dad, I don't even get sick when I eat it," David begged as he looked at his father with his angelic eyes. When David looked at you with those eyes, he could make you do anything, Mark thought to himself.

"Only after breakfast and you better not leave anything on your plate," Mark replied.

"Deal," David said as he reached out his hand and shook his father's hand, with a satisfied look on his face.

"OK buddy drink up," Mark said as he took the glass from the bedside table and gave it to David. David drank the whole thing in one gulp.

"Yuk!" David screamed out as he screwed his face up.

"That's my boy," Mark replied, patting his son on the back.

"I had a dream last night," David said as he tried to ignore the awful taste in his mouth. "It was awesome!" he said in excitement. I saw four people all around my bed praying for me. It was two ladies and two men. One lady was white and the other was black. The black lady looked at me as if she knew me. She told me her name was Jessica. She said I was a very special boy. I really liked her she had such a beautiful smile. The white lady told me her name was Sarah and she kissed me on the cheek. The two guys were so funny Dad. The white man told me his name was Adam and he kept tickling me. The black guy told me his name was James. He picked me up and spun me around. I think they were angels! They said God had a big surprise for me." David said in excitement.

"That sounds like a great dream Davie." Mark replied in amazement.

That is not the best part of the dream Dad! The angels disappeared and all of a sudden I was in the park. I could run and jump. It was great! There was this big red slide, and I was just sliding away."

"What were your Mom and I doing?" his father asked, excited to see his David so happy.

"You guys were not there. I was alone but I didn't mind. I was so happy Dad." Mark could see the light slowly fade from David's eyes. "I wish my dream comes' true Dad," David said with a quiver in his voice.

"I know son I would do anything to make that happen. I would do anything for you," Mark replied as he lovingly embraced his son. He wanted to cheer David up and he thought of a way to do just that. "Hey, it's Saturday and I am not going to work today. How about, you play your Xbox with your old man for the whole day?" Mark asked.

David forced a big smile on his face, but his eyes could not lie. "OK Dad" he replied. Mark could see the forlorn look in his son's eyes and all that he wanted to do was to disappear at that moment. To see the sadness in David's eyes and not be able to do anything about it, felt as if someone was literally tearing his heart from his chest.

"Dad I'm' kind of tired," David said as he started to slide down the bedpost and cover his face with his blanket.

"Alright buddy," Mark replied as he left his son and returned to his own bedroom.

"How is he?" Jennifer asked Mark.

"He's fine, just resting. He told me about the dream he had," Mark replied.

226

"Was it about the three of us?" Jennifer asked as she brushed her beautiful long dark black hair. She sat on her dressing chair and looked at herself in the mirror.

"He was alone," Mark replied. "Playing, healthy as horse and having fun in the park. David wishes his dream could come true and he gave me that look."

"Oh, I hate that look." Sadly, she placed her brush on the dressing table. "The look that says, I am dying inside," She looked down and Mark knew she was about to cry. Jennifer looked up with tears in her eyes and asked. "Are we being punished?"

Mark started to walk towards his wife. As he reached her, he stood behind her chair and placed his arms around her. "God would not do that," he replied lovingly.

"Then why is this happening to our beautiful son?" she cried out. "Is He punishing us for our past sins?"

"Jennifer stop this." He turned her around to face him and looked her straight in her eyes saying with passion, "God loves David more than we do. He didn't do this. You know that."

"If that is the case why is our son sick?" she desperately asked. "Why would God leave David in a place of helplessness and suffering without any help? I am trying to be strong and to keep my faith but it's so hard!" she cried out. "It feels like God gives us enough strength to keep us going but he never takes Davies's pain away!

Why Mark, why?" Jennifer asked as she grabbed on to her husband and sobbed into his chest.

"I don't know," Mark replied softly. He felt as if he was carrying the weight of the world on his shoulders. "All that I can do is keep believing because the alternative is too bleak. I can't hate God. I can't reject him because if I do, I will be lost."

"Aren't we lost now? When will this ever end?" Her cries became louder and louder. "He cries out in pain and vomits his entire meal. Sometimes he struggles to breathe. When is it ever enough!? I just can't bear it!"

"I would do anything for David; I would take his place in a second if I could. I have the strength to do anything I want but my son can't. His weak fragile body won't let him do anything." Mark dishearteningly replied

"That just doesn't seem right or fair," Jennifer's face was covered with fresh tears. She closed her eyes and started praying. "Oh God if you can hear us, please help our son, *please*! There is nothing you can't do. Please don't leave him in so much torment when you can save him. Please don't stay silent anymore. You can choose to stay quiet, leave things as they are but I am begging you to choose to give us a miracle."

Mark joined his wife in prayer. "Dear God, I will do anything for my family, give up everything for my son's happiness. Anything dear Lord. Please help David through this. And Lord, give Jennifer the strength to hold on to her faith. Carry her through this difficult time.

May she feel your presence, your love, and your peace. In Jesus' name we pray, Amen."

Mark reached for the box of tissues on top of the dressing table, taking a bunch of tissues from the box he started to wipe his wife's blotched red face.

"Mark, please forgive me, I don't know what's wrong with me today."

"I understand Jen; we all have weak moments. I know you want to give up on God, but He is all that we have. Even though we don't understand his expression of love, He does love us."
"When I pray, I feel like my heart is covered in barbed wire," Jennifer replied.

"He feels everything we feel," Mark softly replied.

"I feel as if He is so far away, it feels as if I am His least favourite person."

"It feels that way, but it's not true," Mark answered with an encouraging smile. She continued to pour her heart out.

"Sometimes it feels like I am deluding myself. It feels like by believing I am keeping my hope alive, so that I can survive another day but deep inside I know God won't do anything to change things," she said despairingly.

"Do you really believe that?" Mark asked in shock. He didn't know Jennifer was in such a bad space emotionally.

"I do," Jennifer replied softly, but Mark could not say anything. "Under the circumstances you must too," she painfully said.

"Jen if God has turned his back on us, why do I keep praying?"

Jennifer shrugged her shoulders in bewilderment, as another tear escaped from her eye and landed on her check.

"Even when I am so angry and so hurt, I keep praying; I keep coming back to him. That must mean something Jen. God is the one keeping my faith alive even when I push Him away. He is the one not giving up on me," he said emotionally.

"Why does He keep your faith alive when it is hopeless? He does nothing to change things?" she asked helplessly.

"Maybe because it's not time yet."

"Oh, come on Mark. How much more should our son have to take before God decides its time?"

"I don't have all the answers Jen, but I know we are not doing this alone," he lovingly replied as he dropped to his knees and held both her hands. "It may seem like we are walking this rocky mountain alone, but the truth is God is the one carrying us," he continued with passion and conviction. "We are not walking Jen. He is carrying us. No one can survive this alone. We have made it this far because He's been here. It's not over yet; God is not finished with this family that's why He is keeping my hope alive."

"I want to believe you Mark but I am just so tired. David has been sick for so long. I need you, I need your strength," she said desperately.

"You have me. What you need to do, is believe in God again and depend on His strength to see you through. David is not alone, God is with him. He feels and sees everything David is going through, and one day we will understand why we had to go through this."

"I am so blessed to have you as my husband. I don't deserve you," she said softly. Her anger and pain had subsided.

"Jennifer, you, and David are my whole world."

"You're so wonderful, you know that?" she replied.

Mark smiled as he watched a smile start to appear on her face. "How about you make your wonderful husband and son some breakfast?" he lovingly said.

Jennifer smiled and gave Mark a kiss on the cheek. Standing up she put her dressing gown on and walked to David's room.

David was awake, but still in bed leaning on the bedpost. It looked like he was deep in thought.

Chapter 8

"Are you strong enough to join us for breakfast hon?" she asked. "Yes, mom I am having a good day today. I am not feeling sick at all," David replied as he smiled at his mother.

"Good," she said as she tickled her son's tummy.

"Mom, stop!" he cried out and laughed out loud. Jennifer relented to his plea and stopped tickling him. He quickly sat up. "Dad and I are playing on my X box after breakfast," he said in excitement.

"Is that so?"

"Can you play too Mom? After I've beaten Dad for the hundredth time."

"Sure," she lovingly replied.

"He also promised me a slab of chocolate."

"Did he now? How did that happen I wonder?"

"I guess he just loves me," David answered, the smile never leaving his face.

"Or maybe somebody manipulated his way into getting what he wants," she said looking straight into David's eyes with a smile.

"I wonder who would do that," David replied innocently.

"I know you too well Davie," Jennifer suspiciously squinted her eyes. She was about to pounce on and tickle him again, her eyes watching Davie like a tiger ready to attack its victim. Davie knew what his mom was about to do. The doorbell rang at that moment.

Mark walked towards the door and opened it. He was surprised to find an envelope on the ground. Whoever placed the letter on the ground was no longer there, which was very strange, he thought to himself as he picked it up. The letter was in a golden envelope with the word *Destiny* written in italics. Mark quickly opened the envelope and read the letter with curiosity. "Jen, can you come here for a minute?" Mark called out to his wife, who was still in David's room.

"I'll be right there, sweetheart," she said as she quickly kissed David on the forehead and went out of the room. "Mark who was at the door?" she asked while walking towards her husband.

Mark closed the door and went to Jennifer in excitement. "You won't believe this." He did not wait for Jennifer to respond but carried on speaking. "David won a competition!"

"He did what?!" she asked in amazement and utter shock.
"It says he won because has been such loyal customer. The company is going to take the whole family to a tropical island for seven days."

Jennifer's head started to spin. "I need to sit down," she said as she walked to the lounge and sat down. Mark followed her and took a seat next to her. "How do they know about David?"

"I was asked to fill a form every time I bought his favourite chocolate. I wrote David's name and our home address."

"Mark we can't' go," she said protectively. "As soon as he is out of this house, he is going to catch a virus or an infection," she protested.

"Jen, they have David's medical record and history. They know everything," he replied. "They have gone to such lengths of making sure every form of transportation is free from viruses. I am talking about the plane and limo; both are free from viruses."

"But that's so expensive to do," she replied in amazement.

"I know," Mark replied in disbelief. "The island is free from viruses and bacteria! The air is completely clean Jennifer!" said Mark beaming with joy.

"I didn't know such a place existed," she said with tears of joy falling from her eyes. "The air is completely clean?" she asked in shock.

"That's what it says in the letter," Mark replied smiling from ear to ear.

"I can't believe what they are willing to spend on Davie," she said.

"I know the money we spend to keep this house free from viruses is crazy," Mark added.

"It's too good to be true," she replied in astonishment. But she was reluctant to go on the trip and Mark could see that.

"Jen, we need this. We never go anywhere because of David, and we can't go anywhere because every penny we spend is for David. Now we finally can. The trip is absolutely free. Nothing is stopping us. Jen, lets' go," he placed his arm around her waist. "And David's health will not be jeopardised."

Jennifer didn't understand why she was feeling uneasy about going but she didn't want to disappoint Mark or her son. She knew this would make David really happy. She thought to herself, OK let's do it. "I am just being over protective as usual," she uttered.

"Let's go and tell him the good news," Mark said as he took her by the hand and they both stood up from their seats. They found him watching his favourite sitcom in his room, laughing his heart out.

"David, we have good news for you," Jennifer said with a smile. David looked up from the screen with curious eyes.

"What mom?" he asked.

"You tell him," she said as she looked into her husband eyes. She didn't have to ask Mark twice.

Bubbling with excitement Mark exclaimed, "We are going on a trip son."

David's eyes grew bigger. He stood up and asking one question after the other without taking a breath. "What! How!? When are we going?"

"Easy son," Mark replied, trying to calm him down. He went down on his knees and held David's shoulders and said, "Seems like the chocolate slab *Destiny* you like eating so much won you the competition."

David could not contain his excitement and cried out, "Where are we going?"

"To an island," Jennifer said. "We will be staying on a cruise ship for seven days."

"I am going to get to see the ocean!" David screamed.

"And you can feel the sand and water on your feet too," Jennifer replied as she wiped the tears of joy from her eyes.

"Mom, why are you crying?" David asked.

Jennifer bent down on her knees and gave David a big hug. "Because I am so happy for you," she replied.

"When are we going?" David asked.

"Tomorrow," Mark replied with a smile, seeing his son so excited about the trip and Jennifer being so emotional brought tears in his eyes. He quickly blinked and kept the tears from falling. David's face quickly changed. Jennifer and Mark noticed the worried look on his face.
"What's wrong son?" Mark asked.

"Won't I get sick?" David asked.

"No hon, you won't get sick," Jennifer replied in a loving motherly tone. "The island is free of all the bacteria and viruses that make you sick," she explained.
"Really?" David asked in pure astonishment.

"Really," Mark replied with a smile never leaving his face.

"I am so happy!" David screamed out in excitement. Now I know why my favourite chocolate is called *Destiny*. My dream is coming true! God heard my prayers!" David screamed out with joy as he hugged his parents. He fell into their arms, and they tightly held on to him, allowing the tears of joy to freely flow down their faces.

The next day a limo drove the family to the airport and the three of them were flown to the island. The Andersons could not recall disembarking from the plane or ending up on the island. The captivating beauty of the island took priority over everything else and logic had temporarily disappeared as they walked towards the speed boat in a hypnotic state.

It was a magical time that they would never forget, seeing David smile everyday full of glee made Mark and Jennifer joyful. David was not seeing the world through a glass window but through his very eyes. He was no longer sitting on the side lines, but he was a partaker in life. The days were filled with activities, David wanted to experience everything. His health was getting better day by day. If they were not exploring the exotic island, they were either under water deep sea diving or enjoying everything the cruise ship had to offer. Every night was an adventure David wanted to try all the interesting and different restaurants serving mouth-watering cuisines. He wanted to go everywhere and do everything. He enjoyed the games room the most. Jennifer enjoyed everything the spa had to offer from manicures, pedicures, massages to facials and everything else. She also enjoyed shopping for herself and her family in all the designer boutiques on the super-yacht.

On their last night on the island, David had the same experience as James, Sarah, Adam, and Jessica. He was enchanted by the powerful captivating voice, leading him out of his room and out to the deck. Just like the others, David leaned over the deck in a trance and was pulled overboard into the water. He was intrigued not only by the beauty of the sea plants and fish but also by the wooden worn out birdhouse lying on the sand. He felt as if the birdhouse was waiting for him. I am sure you can guess what happened next. Just like the other four, unable to do anything else, David picked up the house and looked deeply into the little window.

He saw himself in the town park, running around the park, riding on the swings playing on the slides and kicking a red ball. The fact that he was alone in the park did not bother him at all. No one else existed in his world. He had no memory of his life with his parents. In his vision, being alone was the only existence he knew. Needing and missing the company of people or to be loved was a foreign language that he did not understand or need to learn. In this world, he was the only person that existed, and David didn't want it any other way. He wanted nothing more than to be in that park and the birdhouse seemed to sense his desire. With every breath he took, the birdhouse drew him into the tiny window, until his legs were the only parts of his body dangling outside.

Fear is a powerful force that keeps you from going after what you want. Are we afraid of breaking the rules, to attain what we desire? Or are we afraid of the consequences of our actions? Or does the fear come from finding out what we desire does not really exist and we are left with the disappointment? David was afraid of letting the birdhouse take him. What if I go inside the house and I am still sick in that world too, he thought to himself. He to pulled himself out of the
house and the same powerful, invoking force pulled him back to the surface. He levitated back to the deck of the ship. The Andersons could not remember boarding or leaving the plane the next day. Their main concern was their son who looked very sad. David thought of nothing else but what he experienced the night before, all through the plane ride back home until the limousine dropped them at their doorstep. Jennifer noticed the difference in

David's mood immediately, but she assumed he was sad the vacation was over.

When David announced that he was going straight to bed without supper. Mark knew something was definitely wrong. Jennifer was the first to speak. "David you hardly had anything for breakfast, and you have been mighty quiet the whole day. Are you upset because the trip is over?" she asked.

David gave them a quick nod and tried to escape to his room. Mark was too fast for him, and he grabbed him by his hand. David was about to burst into tears. "I can't tell you Daddy, please don't make me!" he pleaded.

"Son tell me what's wrong?" Mark said, his voice revealing how worried he was. "Your Mom and I will fix whatever it is I promise," hoping his encouragement would help David tell the truth.

"That's right honey, just tell us what's wrong," Jennifer said anxiously. Before David could respond to their questions, the answering machine made a ringing song indicating someone left a message. The three of them heard David's' voice on the answering machine. He sounded so confident, content and most of all very happy.

"David, come back to the island. You don't have to be afraid. Mom and Dad will be just fine. You know you want to. Your miracle is waiting for you," they heard him say.

Everybody remained completely silent out of sheer shock. Jennifer was the first to break the silence. "What the hell was that!" she exploded.

"Jennifer calm done," Mark said gesturing his head towards his son. Mark picked his son up and walked to the sitting room and placed David on the sofa while sitting beside him. Jennifer could not move an inch, she felt like stone at that moment. Mark understood and didn't say anything; besides, he was more worried about what his son was going to say.

"David what is this about?" he asked trying to be as calm as possible.

"Dad, do you remember the dream I told you about?" David asked cautiously.

"Yes," Mark replied in a natural voice.

"It came true last night," David said as the excitement and wonder quickly started to build from the pit of his tiny stomach.

"I don't understand?" Jennifer replied in utter confusion. She took one step and then another towards the sofa, as she listened to David tell his mystifying wonderful experience.
"I pulled back from the birdhouse because I thought of how you and Mom would miss me. I didn't want to hurt you like that," he said. The relief swept through his body as he finally opened up to his parents.

241

Jennifer could not help but burst into tears as she collapsed on the sofa. "Please Mom, don't cry!" David pleaded with tears in his eyes as he hugged tightly to his mother. "I am never going back to that stupid island ever, ever again."

Mark silently watched his son trying to console his mother while swallowing the lump in his throat. Mark finally picked David up, walked into his room and placed him on his bed. "I want you to stay here for a while. Mom and Daddy need to talk OK," Mark said, trying to be as natural as possible, but his voice betrayed and revealed the turmoil he was feeling inside. David nodded in response. The poor boy was worried about his mother and watched as his father walked out of the room.

As soon as Mark walked back into the sitting room the answering machine made the same familiar ringing sound indicating a message was just about to be heard on the speaker.

"Sometimes love means letting go of someone you love, for them to be happy. This may not be the answer you were waiting for from God but it's the one you received," she heard herself say.

Then they heard Marks voice. "Let him go. David will be healthy and happy here. You said you would do anything if God helped you. This is your anything," he heard himself say.

Then they heard Jennifer's voice again. "He won't remember you as his parents. You know it's the right thing to do, even if it's the

242

hardest thing you have to do." Suddenly the answering machine automatically turned itself off.

"What in God's name is going on here?" Jennifer screeched out of rage and fear. "Mark what we are going to do?" she cried out hysterically.

"I am going to tell you what we are not going to do. We are not going to let our little boy go back to that island!" he screamed out adamantly.

"Now I know why I had this uneasy, sick feeling about going on this trip," Jennifer said as she wiped the tears off her face. "I knew if I let David go, I would regret it for the rest of my life, but I pretended it was nothing," she said with a heavy ache in her heart. "Be careful what you wish for, you might just get it." Jennifer's demeanour completely changed. A strong revelation that caused the faith she thought she had lost in the sea of sorrow, suddenly rose up like an eagle soaring in her heart. She found enlightenment. "Be careful what you ask for, you just might get it." Her whole body felt stiff as Mark reached out to touch her. He was on his knees as he held on to her shaking hands.

"Its OK honey, David is not going anywhere," he said reassuringly.

"We prayed for help, Mark," she said. A tear slid down her face as she looked into his eyes, hoping, and praying he could read between the lines of what she could not say. Mark was not a stupid man. He knew everything about his wife and what every expression meant. He knew exactly what Jennifer was implying. Jennifer knew what she was up against: a father's love for his son.

"This is not God," he seethed in rage, bewildered by what he was hearing. "He would never separate a child from his parents!" Mark continued to yell at his wife as he stood up.

Jennifer kept her composure as she took a picture of David when he was a baby from the side-table. She lovingly looked at the photo as she spoke with a broken heart. "God is above our understanding, Mark. He does things in His own way and time. To us His way never seems right or fair." She placed the picture back on the side-table and stood up. Slowly she walked towards her husband and touched the back of his tense unrelenting shoulder. Mark was taller than she was, so she had to stand on her toes. "Sometimes it doesn't even make sense," she said.

Mark remained silent. It was as if Jennifer was in some form of a trance. Then she said, "His way is gut wrenching. You find yourself wishing for death every day. But when it's over you realize He meant it for your own good. You can't fight or run from God or the plan He has for your life. You accept it and wait for God to finish what he started in your life."

Her soul had found acceptance even though her heart was breaking into a million pieces. "The hardest part is waiting for God to say the test is over, that the growth and maturity He was creating in you has been reached and the lesson was learned. You are waiting for

Him to say it's all over, time for you to smile. God is finally saying it's time for David to smile," she said passionately as she reached for Mark's arm and made him face her. "We have to let him go. This is the time we have to hold on to our faith, Mark, even when everything doesn't make sense," she said as her eyes revealed a sadness that she knew would never go away.

Mark could not believe the words that were coming from her mouth. Jennifer is not thinking straight. The misery of seeing David suffer everyday has driven her insane, he concluded.

"You have lost your damn mind if you think I am going to believe God has any part in this," he said in a harsh tone as he pulled her hands from his arms.

"He has Mark," she replied tenaciously, as Mark viciously pulled her arms from him. "He is doing all of this. Who else could possibly be responsible for this?" she asked.

"The devil!" he answered. "Has that thought crossed your little mind?" he asked in an arrogant tone.

Jennifer was taken aback by Mark's response. He had never used that language or tone with her before. She walked back to the sofa and sat down. Mark was feeling relieved. He thought he had made his point, but he was wrong. Jennifer looked back at him with renewed confidence.

"Do you think the devil would allow our son to be healthy and happy, Mark? Use your head," she said as she stood up. "This has the Almighty written all over it. The God of miracles and you know it!" Mark did not say anything but walked to the window and looked outside. It started to rain. The soft showers represented the tears Mark refused to shed, instead he chose rage. Obscene anger was silently bubbling under the pit of his stomach.

"Come on, Mark," Jennifer continued defiantly. "We are the ones on that machine telling each other to let him go."
"It's a trick!" he screamed out of control as he turned to face her. "And I can't believe you are actually falling for it! You are the one who didn't want him to go to that damn island in the first place! Now you are ready to just give him up? What has happened to you?" he asked, feeling let down by his wife.

Jennifer wanted to die from the look of shame Mark gave her, but she valiantly carried on speaking. "I have changed, Mark, and as painful as this may be, I know it's the right thing to do," she answered.

"Well not for me it isn't!" Mark replied while he held her by her arms and started pushing her towards the sofa. "So you keep your crazy opinions to yourself and never mention that demonic island in this house again!" he screamed, as he flung her on the sofa and quickly turned his back towards her. His anger had turned him irrational, capable of hurting his wife. He had to calm himself down, there was no excuse for this kind of behaviour. Shame ran through his whole body; he could not believe what he had done. Mark could not even bear to look Jennifer in the eyes as he started his apology. "I ...I am sorry Jennifer," he said with a stutter. "I had no right to touch you in that way. Please forgive me but I am not losing my son," he said with difficulty.

It took a few minutes for Jennifer to pull herself together. Mark had never been violent towards her before, she thought to herself. She had almost fallen to the floor when he had pushed her, and it made her whole body shudder. "Mark, he is not happy or healthy here," she answered as she sat up. Mark stayed silent but she carried on speaking. "He is not really living here. David is not going to stay our little boy forever. He is going to grow up and become an angry empty and jaded man. He will lose everything that makes him beautiful and lose his light. You know I am right; you can see the spark fading from his eyes every day. Is that the kind of life you want for him?" she asked firmly.

"No, I don't." Mark said regretfully, his back still turned from her. Jennifer thought she had finally turned a corner with Mark but what he said next hurt her to the very core of her soul.

"So, you are going to abandon your own son?" he said incredulously as he turned to face her.

"No, we are going to do what's right for our son which is to let him go," Jennifer replied as she stood up, taking a brave step towards her husband.

"Never!" he screamed out. The rage from his voice stopped her in her tracks and she did not move in fear. Mark was like a wild animal ready to tear apart anyone and anything that stood in his way.

"Mark please, David will hear you," she said in a trembling voice. Mark was out of control, and he knew it. He flung himself on the sofa as he tried to simmer down. He noticed David's picture on the side-table and picked it up. Looking at his son's face finally brought tears to his eyes.

"I am not going give up my son," he replied in agony.
"You promised you would do anything for him, Mark," she reminded him. The tables had turned, Jennifer had developed a deep strength that made her encourage her husband, comforting him as she went on her knees holding on to her husband's trembling hands.
"I meant walking through fire or sacrificing my life but not this," he said as he swallowed hard. Anything but this," he said with desperation. " Anything means anything Mark," she replied gently.

His eyes turned to steel. "How can you be so cold?" he replied in shock.

The judgement in her husband's voice was something she could not take.
"There is nothing more heart wrenching, than to see your child suffer and lose a piece of himself every day," she said defensively. "Did you see the joy in his eyes when he was telling us the story?" she asked. The truth kept Mark silent, and he could feel himself starting to lose control again. Jennifer continued speaking. "He wants to go Mark, with everything in him. But he won't because he knows what it will do to us," she said fervently. She was desperate for Mark to see reason, but he would not budge. He did not utter

a single word trying to suppress his anger. "He is willing to sacrifice his own happiness for us! We are his parents; we should sacrifice our own happiness for his. We should be the ones making the hard decisions, not keep him prisoner! " She pleaded.

"Enough. I have had enough of this!" he shouted. David was not a prisoner. Who was this woman and where was his wife? he asked himself. "David does not want to go and I will prove it to you," he said with outrageous fury and stood up. "What kind of mother are you anyway?" he asked scornfully.

"A good one!" Jennifer said indignantly. She was irate and as the tears spilled over her face, she felt her anger surging through her body. Jennifer could not take one more cruel word coming out of Mark's mouth. She had lost her patience. She wiped the angry tears from her eyes.

"Yeah, right," he answered mockingly.

Jennifer gave him a death stare, and could not utter a single word. She was livid. Mark undeterred by the stare, marched straight into his son's room, he picked David up and walked back to the sitting room. Jennifer was still sitting on the couch. Mark placed David between Jennifer and himself.

"David, did you overhear Mommy and Daddy talking" Jennifer asked out of concern.

"No, Mom," David lied, giving his mother a smile that said everything he could not say. Thanking her for being his champion.

"If you could not remember us, would you go to the island?" Mark asked him.

"No Daddy," David replied honestly. Mark gave Jennifer a satisfied victorious look.
Jennifer was not moved. "David if we had no memory of you as our son, would you go back to the island?" she carefully asked.

David kept silent, unable to divulge what was in his heart. Mark could see how difficult it was for David to answer.

"Don't be afraid son, it's OK to tell the truth," he said reassuringly. David slowly nodded as he looked down, avoiding any eye contact with his father. A feeling of vindication spread across Jennifer's face as she looked at her husband. He could not run from the truth anymore, she concluded.

"Thank you, son, you are my brave boy. You can go back to your room now," Mark said with a lump in his throat. David obeyed his father and quietly walked back to his room.

"I want him to be happy," Mark said as his voice broke. "I love David," he continued to say. He could not fight anymore. He knew he had to let David go. "I just didn't think making him happy meant losing him," he said.

David's Escape

"If we don't act now David will fade away until there is nothing left of his soul," Jennifer replied sadly.

"You are talking about abandoning our son," he said as a tear drop escaped his eye.

"No, I am talking about setting him free from an unfulfilling life," she answered with conviction.

"How are we going to live without him?" Mark asked as he laid his head on to his wife's lap and started to cry like a baby.

"I don't know, but we will learn somehow," she replied as she lovingly placed her hand on his cheek. He nodded as another tear escaped from his eyes. "We will take his pain and make it ours," she said. Jennifer had won. Mark was going to let David go. Jennifer realised what her triumph over her husband meant. She was going to live without her David and suddenly something deep inside started to ache. Sometimes God will give you this one precious thing. This gift you have always dreamed of. Suddenly your love for this gift eclipses any love you have felt before and then He takes it away, she quietly reflected. The tears moved down her checks silently.

"We will tell him we won't remember him as our son as soon as he leaves the house," Mark said choking up.

"It's a lie, but it's a good lie," she said agreeing with her husband.

Chapter 8

Mark stood up and turned the radio on. *Clair de lune* by Debussy filled the room. He turned the volume high hoping the music would muffle the sound of their tears as he walked back to his wife. They held on to each other, their tears mingling together. Mark and Jennifer's unrelenting tears had replaced words as they held on to each other tightly.

The time for the lie came sooner than they thought. David could not sleep and went back to the sitting room. Fortunately, Mark and Jennifer heard his footsteps coming and in an instance the tears were replaced by huge smiles on their faces. You could hardly believe that these two had been crying. It was the performance of a lifetime.

"Can I come in?" David asked anxiously as he entered the room.

"Of course, honey come and sit between us," Jennifer replied. David quickly obeyed his mothers' instructions.

"We have great news for you," Mark said as he looked into David's loving eyes.

"What?" David asked in concern.

"You don't have to worry about hurting our feelings anymore, David. Mom and I want you to go back to the island," Mark said as he pushed his pain deep inside.

"But what about you and Mom?"

"We are going to be just fine. When you leave this house, the island is going to erase our memories and we won't remember that we ever had a son," she assuredly answered in her motherly tone.

David was confused by what his mother was saying. "But how?" he asked.
"Well, it's a very special island and has such special powers," Mark replied and took his son's hand.

"Nothing is stopping you from going back to the island now," Jennifer said as she reached for David's other hand, her smile never leaving her face for a second.

"Really?" David asked in disbelief.

"Yes son," Mark replied.

"Then I can go. I want to go back with all my heart!" David said in excitement. He didn't even take a breath as he carried on talking. "I want to run, kick a ball, play in the park and never ever get sick! Thanks Mom and Dad you're the best parents in the whole world." Tears of joy filled David's eyes as he held on to his parents, hugging them both for as long as he possibly could.

"You're welcome my love," Jennifer replied as she wiped one tear drop from her cheek.

"I would do anything for you, son," Mark said and David gave him the biggest grin in return.

Chapter 8

The sun started to descend and hide from the world. "Well, it's getting late, and I should start cooking," Jennifer said. She was about to get up from her seat, but Mark stopped her.

"How about we break tradition, let's have pizza, play games and have lots and lots of fun tonight!" Mark said enthusiastically. Jennifer realized it was the last night they were going to have with their son and Mark wanted to make it special, by doing everything David loved to do, to have a memory that would last forever in their minds. She had never loved Mark more than she did at that moment.

"I think that's a brilliant idea. She lovingly answered. It was truly a special night for the Anderson family as they played video games and ate pizza. Mark and Jennifer allowed David to win each game. You could not remove the sunlit smile from David's face. Jennifer fetched David's photo album and they looked at the pictures, each photograph possessing a memory of David's life since he was a little baby. Each image containing a story they were just too eager to tell him. They took countless photo shots with their son that night.

David kept asking, "Why do you keep taking pictures of me if you are going to forget me?"

"It's just a habit," Jennifer lied.

"I will delete the pictures before we go to bed," Mark answered protecting his son from the painful truth.

David was just too giddy with delight to suspect anything. The pillow fights they had were a bitter sweet memory for Mark and

Jennifer, but they carried on the pretence. Those were the memories that would carry them through the dark days to come.

The night slipped away, and morning came. David had no recollection of who his parents were, as Jennifer washed and dressed him. It was a strange breakfast since he called his parents "Ma'am and Sir." Jennifer and Mark stayed strong, not a single tear drop was seen on their faces. Not even when they hugged him and said goodbye. It was all smiles as David climbed into the white limo that was taking him to the airport and drove away with him at six in the morning.

He waved goodbye as he smiled to the strangers that were his parents. Only when the limo disappeared from their eyesight with their son, did the tears come.

"What will we tell people?" Jennifer cried out.

"The truth, that he is no longer with us," Mark replied as he reached out for her and held on tightly.

"They will think he died," Jennifer answered as she cried on his shirt.

"We will tell everyone the trip was just too much for him and his little body couldn't take it anymore," Mark replied as he wept.
"Lets' say that we cremated his body and scattered his ashes at the island, " she said as she dissolved into tears.

Chapter 8

The limo reached the airport on time. The air hostess led David to his seat on the plane and once again David was taken back to the island. He fell into a tranquil sleep and woke up as the aircraft landed on the island. David's feet touched the white sand as he walked slowly out of the plane towards a calm turquoise sea. Each step taking him closer to his future, to everything he had been anticipating and dreaming of. His eyes never looking away from what was before him, excitement running through him. David knew his life would never be the same again, bringing him closer to his destiny. Each step he took, promised a new tomorrow and the leaving of a sad past. Finally, his feet felt wet, David moved further and deeper into the ocean until his feet could not feel the ground beneath him. David felt an extraordinary sensational force pull his feet until he reached the bottom of the ocean.

The birdhouse lay on the ground, David picked up the birdhouse and looked deep into the little window, as he did before. The birdhouse claimed David as its own possession and slowly his tiny body disappeared through the small window. The mysterious birdhouse floated back down to the sandy ocean floor, waiting for another unsuspecting soul to save. Could that soul, be you?

Jennifer and Mark did not survive their loss by forgetting David. But it was through loving him that they lived. Trying to resist the love they had for their son was the reason they could not move on, but surrendering to that love was the only answer. Mark and Jennifer poured out every ounce of love they had for David to their friends, family, and the community. It made them better people in more ways than one. The secret was not to run from what they were feeling, but to own it and make it part of who they were now. Mark and Jennifer grew into who God destined them to be. Loving David would always be part of who they were. The grief they were feeling was converted into kindness. The Andersons visited and supported orphanages, old age homes and went to missions all over the world building houses and schools for the poor. Every smile came from a sincere and genuine place but Jennifer's eyes carried the sadness of losing her son like a cup carries water.

Three years flew by and the Andersons were blessed with a little bundle of joy called Hope. She was a beautiful healthy baby girl.

She tended to be restless early in the morning. Jennifer liked to listen to music in the sitting room when she breastfed her. Mark was awake and, in the kitchen, looking for something to eat during this time. He took a fresh mango from the fridge, peeled it, and took a nice juicy bite. He walked to Jennifer and gently held the mango close to her lips and fed it to her. Mark sat beside his wife as the TV screen turned on automatically. David was on the television screen, playing in the town park. At last David was free from everything that held him bound for so long. He was free from sickness, free from pain and free from loneliness and alive for the very first time. Marks' heart lapped with joy as he watched his son playing his little heart out. They watched him on the swing, kicking a red ball and going on slides. It was a wonderful sight to see. In this world time did not exist, David played for as long as he wanted. He never grew tired or hungry. He stayed young, playing forever in his eternal playground.

Chapter 8

The TV screen turned off automatically and they smiled with tears in their eyes. David was fine, more than fine, and that was all that mattered. Sometimes doing the right thing comes with a price and that price is usually your heart, Jennifer thought to herself as she and Mark fawned over their little girl.

Now you know about Jessica, Adam, James, and Sarah. You also know about the Andersons and little Davie. You know about the island and the mysterious birdhouse and how the impossible can happen. Your dreams are never lost forever; they find their way back home to you.

THE END.

*L*ife can sometimes bring us to our knees and we actually believe that we are unloved and God does not care what happens to us. So we choose to walk a different path and have nothing to do with Him, or maybe you once had a relationship with God but backslide. I want you to know that God's love for you is unending and fulfilling. He can heal you from every wound that has been inflicted on your soul. He is ready to welcome you with open arms. If you are ready to start this journey with Him. Say this prayer after me.

Lord Jesus I know you are the son of God, who was crucified and died on the cross because of my sins. On the third day you rose from the dead. I repent of my sins. Come into my heart. I make you my Lord and Savior. Amen. If you said this prayer I believe you have been born again, please look for a good Bible based church in your area.